Jodi,

Merry Christmas
2003!

Love Chris

Abounding
Grace

Abounding Grace

AN ANTHOLOGY
OF WISDOM

EDITED, WITH COMMENTARY, BY

M. Scott Peck, M.D.

ARIEL BOOKS
Andrews McMeel
Publishing

Acknowledgment

Since the single largest number of quotes in this anthology were gathered from *Lessons at the Halfway Point: Wisdom for Midlife* by Michael Levine, I would specifically like to thank my friend, Michael, for donating them to this work. They are, however, copyrighted by him, and are not for general use without his permission.

Frontispiece illustration © 1996 Christopher Peck

Book design by Maura Fadden Rosenthal / Mspaceny

00 01 02 03 04 RDH 10 9 8 7 6 5 4 3 2 1

Library of Congress Cataloging-in-Publication Data

Abounding grace : an anthology of wisdom / edited by M. Scott Peck.
    p. cm.
    "Ariel books."
    ISBN 0-7407-1014-1
    1. Self-realization—Quotations, maxims, etc. 2. Virtues—Quotations, maxims, etc. 3. Conduct of life—Quotations, maxims, etc. I. Peck, M. Scott (Morgan Scott), 1936–

PN6084.S45 A25 2000
082—dc21   00-029325

contents

preface

The genesis of this volume was the inspiration of Armand Eisen. Armand, president and founder of Ariel Books, is a sort of impresario in the publishing world. He gets things started. Then he sits back to watch what happens.

Over the years Armand and his staff gathered a compendium of some forty-five hundred quotes about seventy-nine different virtues. In January 1997, he then asked me if I would care to edit his compendium. A lot has happened since.

I looked at the compendium. It was, for the most part, boring—as compendiums tend to be. Yet it had potential. I told Armand that if I were to edit it there would have to be radical changes. He gave me free rein, and that is how I became an editor for the first time in my life.

The radical changes were really only two, but they were big ones.

The lesser change was that although I kept Armand's seventy-nine virtues, I organized them into twelve broader categories or parts. Then for each of those parts I have written a few words of introduction—words that seemed to me to add a note of clarification.

For example, the first part is on the virtue of happiness, but within this section I have included other virtues such as humor, contentment, and forgiveness. In my remarks about happiness I refer to these others as "component virtues," because they seem to me to be necessary components of happiness. And so it will go in regard to each of the sections.

The more significant change is that I deleted the vast majority of Armand's quotes, reducing their number from forty-five hundred down to approximately sixteen hundred even after adding a few of my own favorites that his compendium had overlooked.

What this meant was that the book went through a metamorphosis from a compendium into an anthology. A compendium strives for completeness so it can be used as a reference work, like a dictionary. An anthology does not so strive; it is a selection, based solely on the individual taste of the editor. Consequently, what you have here are my favorite quotations about virtue.

Please do not be angry with me if I have failed to include some of your favorite quotations. There are two possibilities. One is simply that Armand and I were not familiar with your favorites. The other possibility is that I deselected yours because our tastes differ. That doesn't mean that my taste is better than yours; only different.

Editing this anthology has made me aware, far more than I was before, of the reasons that a phrase or sentence or two might be particularly quotable. I've even started to compose a few of my own quotes as a result. For instance, having just remarked that our human tastes naturally differ I might still pronounce: "Taste, when good, is not necessarily a matter of mere subjectivity. It may be quite rational."

So let me offer some of the reasons I have excluded certain quotes while including others.

I excluded a great many because they struck me as simplistic, and therefore lacking in wisdom. By way of example, it is commonly said: "Tolerance is a virtue." This is the sort of quote I deleted. Although tolerance may often be a virtue, the fact is there are many varieties of human behavior that should not be tolerated, and whole societies have gone to ruin because they tolerated the intolerable. Conversely, I included virtually all those quotes that smacked of paradox. For me, the capacity to embrace paradox—to perceive the validity of opposites, such as tolerance and intolerance, each in its own season—is a key to wisdom.

I excluded a large number of quotes that seemed to me excessively wordy or convoluted. This meant excluding much great poetry of figures like Milton or Wordsworth. Instead, I tended to gravitate toward the pithy.

Although most of my inclusions are quite serious, I found in myself a preference for the humorous. Indeed, one of the seventy-nine virtues covered is that of humor. Paradoxically, of course, there can be "good" and "bad" humor, but I believe we need all the good humor we can get, and the more the merrier.

Proverbs are such because they are containers of wisdom. Nonetheless, I have excluded many proverbs of our own culture since they are so familiar as to seem trite (although I have retained a few so important that they can bear the burden of being "old saws"). On the other hand, I have included quite a few proverbs from foreign cultures not only because they are wise but also because they sound fresh to our ears.

Finally, I have included some quotations for the simple beauty of their passion. It is another common saying that "Beauty is in the eye of the beholder." This brings me back to the distinct possibility that although I might think my taste utterly reasonable, others may have reason to doubt it. Please doubt away.

introduction

Since the quotes herein are organized according to different virtues, I would like to say some words about the subject of virtue in general. And this means we must return to the subject of paradox, for all virtues are paradoxical.

Every blessing can be a potential curse and every virtue a potential vice. I have already spoken of good and bad humor. Let me elaborate by telling you about the funniest man I've ever known. I'll call him Harry—a pseudonym to protect his identity.

Lily, my wife, and I became friends with Harry instantly upon meeting him, the pleasure of his company was so great. Many times he kept us in stitches throughout the evening with his brilliant wit. It was not long, however, before we sensed underneath his humor a deep sadness. Or was it depression? We commented about this. Harry made a big joke of it, so we dropped the matter for months.

But after those months Harry's humor became increasingly biting and sarcastic, even to the point of occasionally being crude. This time I confronted him frankly, suggesting that he seek psychotherapy. Again he did his best to make a joke of it. "Harry, you're hiding behind your sense of humor," I told him. "You're using it not only to defend against your depression but also to defend your depression—to protect it. This is what many professional comedians do. You know we appreciate how funny you are, but it's getting to be too much of a good thing. Stop joking. Get some help."

It didn't work, of course.

Shortly thereafter my job forced us to move to the other end of the country. Lily and I were actually relieved that the move interrupted our friendship with Harry. His "funniness" had entirely ceased to be uplifting.

A year later the phone rang in the middle of the night. It was Harry, calling from the locked ward of his local psychiatric hospital to which he'd been remanded by the judge after an arrest for bizarre, extremely destructive criminal behavior. He reported this as if it were yet another amusing story. I asked if there was some way I might be of assistance. There wasn't, he responded. Bored in "the loony bin," he'd merely called "to kid around a bit." I gently reminded him that it was 3:00 A.M. on the East Coast. He was unfazed. So I gave him what he wanted because he wouldn't receive what was needed: I joked around with him for half an hour before I managed to get him to say good-bye, and eventually I got back to sleep.

It was a good-bye. I never heard from Harry again. I've wondered what became of him, but I am not sure I want to know. The only homage I've paid to our brief friendship has been to pray for him now and then.

I noted in this anthology that humor is a virtue, specifically, one of the components of happiness. This is because I know I personally am unable to bear even the most minor vicissitudes of this life without relying upon whatever sense of humor I possess. I also rely upon my friends. And I don't have any friends totally lacking a sense of humor. I find humorless people very hard to take.

But as the case of Harry indicates, a sense of humor cannot guarantee sustained friendship or meaningful happiness. Indeed, carried to excess, it can alienate friends and obstruct happiness—your own and that of others. The same pattern is true of all but one of the virtues (the only exception being that of wisdom). Carried too far, thrift becomes miserliness and compassion produces waste. The great ancient Greek prescription for virtue was "Nothing in excess." Specifically this was a prescription for moderation—another one of our seventy-nine virtues. Even this is paradoxical, however. Moderation itself can be carried to an extreme, and an excess of it will turn itself into multiple vices: dullness, humorlessness, a lack of passion, and ultimately a loss not only of spontaneity but even humanity.

A sense of humor is further typical of all the other virtues in that I have no idea from whence it comes. If everybody had one, we probably wouldn't even consider it a virtue; it would just be a given part of human nature. But the fact of the matter is that a substantial minority of human beings seem truly devoid of any sense of humor whatsoever. Why? Is a sense of humor the result of a gene that some inherit and others don't, according to the luck of a Mendelian draw? Is it something that we absorb in early childhood from our parents and the other role models of our primary culture? Or is it something we learn only as we continue to age over decades of dealing with the exigencies of life? I honestly don't know. I suspect, to one degree or another, it is the result of all of the above and more. Curse me for my vagueness, if you will, but as far as I can ascertain, the entire profession of psychology shares my ignorance.

There is an expression frequently made about a particular "talent" that we can also make about a particular virtue. We customarily refer to a talent for writing, drawing, playing the violin, or even making money, as a "gift." I would not distinguish at all between talents and virtues in this regard. I believe that a sense of humor, for instance, is a gift. On one level this explains absolutely nothing. Although it suggests that some are given this talent or virtue whereas others are given that one, the notion of a gift doesn't clarify whether it is given to us by our genes, our parents, ourselves, or even by God. The notion does, however, tend to nurture "an attitude of gratitude." And gratitude I have also categorized as one of the other component virtues of happiness. Furthermore, as I have written elsewhere, "the capacity to perceive our own virtues and other blessings as gifts is itself a gift."

Twenty years ago, while beginning research for a book on evil, I happened to read two authors on the subject of "The Seven Deadly Sins." Although otherwise vastly different volumes, each made the same point: The major sins are all interconnected.

Although it is an ambiguous notion, consider "original sin." Mythologically, the concept is derived from Genesis 3, the story of how the serpent beguiled Adam and Eve to eat the fruit of the Tree of Knowledge of Good and Evil despite the fact that God had commanded them not to eat it. In pondering why this disobedience might have been such a sin, it occurred to me that God may have been in the habit of strolling through the Garden of Eden, routinely conversing with the pair. If so, how was it that Adam and Eve hadn't asked, "Hey, God, *why* don't you want us to eat the fruit?" I began to wonder if the great sin was not so much disobedience as the failure to ask questions of God (or Life).

Why this failure? The story is mute about the matter. But I can think of at least three possible answers. One is that Adam and Eve were too proud, thinking perhaps, "Who's God to boss us around? We can be our own gods." Another is that they were too fearful—afraid not so much of God (He had seemed pleasant enough up until then) but afraid of what He might reply. Finally, they might have simply been too lazy to go to the trouble of dialoguing with Him (or Her). Which was it? Pride? Fear? Sloth? Each is one of the seven deadly sins. My own supposition is that it was a mixture of all three and more.

Not only are the major sins intertwined, but any one of them tends to beget the others. Commit a serious indiscretion because of any one sin, for instance, and you'll be likely to attempt to cover it up by lying—which is yet another sin. Sin breeds sin.

And virtue breeds virtue. All that I've said about the sins holds true for the virtues. Courage tends to beget honesty. Gratitude tends to beget contentment. This is perhaps the reason for the saying (so trite it's one of the quotes I've excluded), "Virtue is its own reward."

Moreover, like sins, the virtues tend to be so intertwined that it is almost impossible to tease one of them apart from another. Not only are humor and gratitude components of happiness, but so also is forgiveness. And forgiveness may be rooted in charity and compassion—which are close to synonyms for love.

One of the things this means is that the delineation of the seventy-nine virtues herein, and their categorization into twelve sections, border upon the arbitrary. This has not been done thoughtlessly, however. To speak about any subject as large as virtue, one must divide it into components for coherency. And arbitrary though this division might seem at times, it will be of at least some slight help in locating a particular quote. A saying about God, for instance, is most likely to be found in the part on faith. Still, everything is related, and you may have to look for it in the section on purity. Or on love. Or . . .

Speaking of faith, you will find many of the introductions to the sections that follow have a certain Christian flavor. This is no accident. In my late thirties I gradually—almost reluctantly—began to designate myself as a Christian, a designation I finally formalized with my baptism at the age of forty-three.

An early reader of these introductions commented: "I did find myself perplexed by many of your religious references. Sometimes you speak as a Catholic, sometimes as a Calvinist, and sometimes in another Christian guise. . . . I wonder if others . . . might find this confusing." Again, her finding is no accident. I was baptized by a Methodist minister in an Episcopalian convent through a ceremony deliberately designed to be nondenominational, and I have jealously guarded my nondenominational status ever since.

Furthermore, I was ever so slowly nurtured toward my Christian baptism by all the wisdom I found in the mystical traditions of Hinduism, Buddhism, Taoism, Judaism, and Islam. I have no desire to disavow these traditions, and you may find herein some flavors of them as well. As a Christian, I am not only nondenominational but highly ecumenical. I do not believe that Christianity has a monopoly on wisdom.

Saving it for the conclusion of this introduction, I sneakily neglected to mention the most important criterion for my selection of the quotes herein. As often as not I selected those that particularly caused me to think.

This was a criterion because, for me, thinking is the most virtuous activity of all. Yet thinking has not been included as one of the virtues. The reason for this is my belief that it undergirds all of the others. Who would not declare thoughtfulness to be a virtue? Love one another and you will be thoughtful of each other; you will be considerate. Shepherd your resources, and you will do so thoughtfully. Who has heard of thoughtless tactfulness? I could go on and on.

This is an anthology of wisdom. To some indefinable extent, like the other virtues, wisdom is a gift. Certain people seem to be almost born with an instinct for wisdom. On the other hand, I also believe that wisdom can be learned, but only by thinking about the challenges and experiences of our lives.

I suspect that most people, if asked, would proclaim love to be the greatest of the virtues. But I am not so sure. There is no question that love will make many more thoughtful—that love is the force propelling them to stretch their minds on be-half of their beloved. Yet I know of many instances where by thinking deeply, women and men have been led to become more empathetic, more compassionate, more loving. It is un-clear to me whether there is not enough love in the world or whether there is not enough good thinking. As I think about it, however, it is not an either/or matter. Rather we might sup-pose that these two—real love and real thinking—go hand in hand, operating in tandem.

In any case, a large number of the following quotations had the effect of causing me to think, to stretch my mind a bit. It is my hope that they will serve you in the same way.

—M. SCOTT PECK

PART I

HAPPINESS

Unquestionably, it is human nature to desire happiness, at any time and at any place.

This desire, this inherent part of us, may also be the root of what Christian theologians call original sin. Why else would Adam and Eve have disobeyed God by eating the forbidden fruit of the Tree of the Knowledge of Good and Evil unless they thought they might somehow become even happier as a result?

I am often asked why I began my first book with the sentence: "Life is difficult." My answer is always, "Because I wanted to combat the Lie."

The Lie is that we are here on earth to be comfortable, happy, and fulfilled. Is that not our very purpose for being? Certainly it is the message with which we are bombarded by the media every possible minute, catering to our original sin by suggesting that if we're not feeling comfortable, happy, or fulfilled, then something must be terribly wrong: We must not own the right car; we must not be eating the right cereal; or worst of all, we must not have it right with God.

The truth is that our finest moments are most likely to occur when we are feeling deeply uncomfortable, unhappy, or unfulfilled. For it is only in such moments, propelled by our discomfort, that we are likely to step out of our ruts and start searching for different ways or truer answers—or even for God.

William James defined generic religion (or spirituality, if you will) as "the attempt to be in harmony with an unseen order of things." Among the quotes that follow, Henry Miller (an author more renowned for sexuality than spirituality) strangely echoes James when he says: "The world is not to be put in order; the world is in order. It is for us to put ourselves in unison with this order."

Although both Miller and James imply that being in harmony with this invisible order is a secret—perhaps *the* secret—to happiness, neither of them intended it to sound like a simple matter. The order is, after all, invisible and hence inevitably mysterious, as well as beyond manipulation. It is often not what we think it is and certainly often not what we want it to be. Yet it does give us hints of itself, revelations, although not necessarily according to our schedule. It (God, to me) even occasionally speaks to us through that "still, small voice." And one of the things I myself have heard it say repeatedly is: "There's more to life than happiness."

For example, one of the components of happiness, listed here as a virtue in its own right, is contentment. Fine, but does God or the unseen order want us to be content with murder? With rape? With slavery? With a caste system or any other systematic form of oppression? No! And so, paradoxically, there is something we have come to correctly call "divine discontent."

Ah, paradox, as always. There are at least two sides to everything. Having decried the desire for happiness as the possible root of original sin, let me now extol it as the possible root of "original virtue." Was it a bad thing that Adam and Eve developed the knowledge of good and evil and were cast out of the womb of Eden? In the long run, I think not.

I proclaimed that our finest moments more often than not are occasions of profound unhappiness, of "divine discontent." Why is this so? It is because our desire for happiness propels us into situations of unhappiness to rectify the situation. Sometimes our attempts at rectification are bumbling, even fatal. Drug abuse or suicide are examples. At other times, however, our attempts at rectification are noble. The result may be repentance or conversion to a more spiritual life—or some other form of personal healing and *change*. Possibly even grand social change. Whether its cause was the unhappiness of simple fatigue or of victimization I do not know, but I do know it was divine discontent that gave Rosa Parks the courage to refuse to move to the back of the bus that afternoon in December 1955.

So, by all means, seek happiness. But do so wisely. Conflicting though they may sometimes seem, the quotes that follow offer many clues for success in finding the necessary wisdom.

The idea that happiness as an unmodified goal will likely be self-defeating keeps popping up. Seek to be loved and you probably won't be; seek to love, on the other hand, and you probably will be. Look solely for happiness, and I doubt you'll find it. Forget about happiness, seek wisdom and goodness, and probably happiness will find you. Happiness is usually indirect, a side effect or by-product of something else.

What "something else"? No one thing. The component virtues that follow—acceptance, cheerfulness, contentment, forgiveness, humor, serenity and, above all, gratitude—are all such other things, and therefore clues. You cannot be fully happy, for instance, if there is someone in your life you currently hate. Yet there are twists and turns. Some of the quotes acknowledge the reality that it is necessary to judge a man guilty of a crime before it is possible to genuinely pardon him. All else is what I have labeled "cheap forgiveness." Forgiveness is the relinquishment of anger. There can be no real forgiveness without there first being real and righteous anger. If not held onto for too long, righteous "holy" anger is one of the most God-given of emotions.

Finally, as I suggested in the introduction, the virtues must work hand in hand, sometimes smoothly "in synch" and sometimes out of the conflicting turmoil of agonizing over what is right and what is wrong, each in its own place and time.

In this section there is a focus upon acceptance and serenity. In the next section the focus will be upon courage. In the end wisdom. They are all necessary ingredients of the same stew. Nowhere is this more clear than in the famed Serenity Prayer, popularized by the Twelve Step Program but attributed to the theologian, Reinhold Niebuhr:

> *O God, grant me the serenity*
> *To accept the things I cannot change,*
> *The courage to change the things I can,*
> *And the wisdom to know the difference.*

acceptance

I accept the universe!
> — MARGARET FULLER

There are people who live lives little different than the beasts, and I don't mean that badly. I mean that they accept whatever happens day to day without struggle or question or regret. To them things just are, like the earth and sky and seasons.
> — CELESTE DE BLASIS

Everything in life that we really accept undergoes a change.
> — KATHERINE MANSFIELD

When we have accepted the worst, we have nothing more to lose. And that automatically means—we have everything to gain.
> — DALE CARNEGIE

God does not make clones. Each person is different, a tribute to God's creativity. If we are to love our neighbors as ourselves, we must accept people as they are and not demand that they conform to our own image.
> — HENRY FEHREN

If a man does not keep pace with his companions, perhaps it is because he hears a different drummer. Let him step to the music which he hears, however measured or far away.
— HENRY DAVID THOREAU

You must shift your sail with the wind.
— ITALIAN PROVERB

It just ain't possible to explain some things. It's interesting to wonder on them and do some speculation, but the main thing is you have to accept it—take it for what it is, and get on with your growing.
— JIM DODGE

Growth begins when we start to accept our own weakness.
— JEAN VANIER

I didn't belong as a kid, and that always bothered me. If only I'd known that one day my differentness would be an asset, then my early life would have been much easier.
— BETTE MIDLER

Learn not to sweat the small stuff.
— DR. KENNETH GREENSPAN

If you can alter things, alter them. If you cannot, put up with them.
— ENGLISH PROVERB

Do you know why that cow looks over that wall? . . . She looks over the wall because she cannot see through it, and that is what you must do with your troubles—look over and *above* them.
— JOHN WESLEY

We all may have come on different ships, but we're in the same boat now.
— MARTIN LUTHER KING JR.

Acceptance is not submission; it is acknowledgment of the facts of a situation. Then deciding what you're going to do about it.
— KATHLEEN CASEY THEISEN

You have to take it as it happens, but you should try to make it happen the way you want to take it.
— GERMAN PROVERB

Argue for your limitations, and sure enough, they're yours.
— RICHARD BACH

First ask yourself: What is the worst that can happen? Then prepare to accept it. Then proceed to improve on the worst.
— DALE CARNEGIE

God asks no man whether he will accept life. This is not the choice. You must take it. The only question is how.
— HENRY WARD BEECHER

To repel one's cross is to make it heavier.
— HENRI FRÉDÉRIC AMIEL

There are two ways of meeting difficulties: you alter the difficulties, or you alter yourself to meet them.
— PHYLLIS BOTTOME

Arrange whatever pieces come your way.
— VIRGINIA WOOLF

Life is not always what one wants it to be, but to make the best of it, as it is, is the only way of being happy.
— JENNIE JEROME CHURCHILL

True freedom lies in the realization and calm acceptance of
the fact that there may very well be no perfect answer.
—ALLEN REID McGINNIS

Anything in life that we don't accept will simply make
trouble for us until we make peace with it.
—SHAKTI GAWAIN

I have accepted fear as a part of life—specifically the fear of
change. . . . I have gone ahead despite the pounding in
the heart that says: turn back . . .
—ERICA JONG

You are responsible for your life. You can't keep blaming
somebody else for your dysfunction. . . . Life is really
about moving on.
—OPRAH WINFREY

Life is not so much a problem to be solved as a mystery to be
lived.
—ANONYMOUS

cheerfulness

I have always preferred cheerfulness to mirth. The latter I
consider as an act, the former as an habit of mind. Mirth
is short and transient, cheerfulness fixed and permanent.
— JOSEPH ADDISON

The best part of health is fine disposition.
— RALPH WALDO EMERSON

A good-natured man has the whole world to be happy out of.
— ALEXANDER POPE

Few are qualified to shine in company, but it is in most men's
power to be agreeable.
— JONATHAN SWIFT

There is nothing more beautiful than cheerfulness in an old
face.
— JEAN PAUL RICHTER

I felt an earnest and humble desire, and shall do till I die, to
increase the stock of harmless cheerfulness.
— CHARLES DICKENS

A happy woman is one who has no cares at all; a cheerful woman is one who has cares but doesn't let them get her down.
— BEVERLY SILLS

Cheerfulness, it would appear, is a matter which depends fully as much on the state of things within, as on the state of things without and around us.
— CHARLOTTE BRONTË

A cheerful temper, joined with innocence will make beauty attractive, knowledge delightful, and wit good-natured.
— JOSEPH ADDISON

I am still determined to be cheerful and happy in whatever situation I may be, for I have also learned from experience that the greater part of our happiness or misery depends on our dispositions and not on our circumstances.
— MARTHA WASHINGTON

Keep a green tree in your heart and perhaps the singing bird will come.
— CHINESE PROVERB

The best way to cheer yourself up is to try to cheer somebody else up.
— MARK TWAIN

Cheerfulness, in most cheerful people, is the rich and satisfying result of strenuous discipline.
— EDWIN PERCY WHIPPLE

Cheerfulness is contagious, but don't wait to catch it from others. Be a carrier!
— ANONYMOUS

contentment

Be content with your lot; one cannot be first in everything.
— AESOP

Content may dwell in all stations. To be low, but above contempt, may be high enough to be happy.
— SIR THOMAS BROWNE

Better a little fire to warm us than a great one to burn us.
— THOMAS FULLER, M.D.

fat hens lay few eggs.

— GERMAN PROVERB

Oh, don't the days seem lank and long,
When all goes right and nothing goes wrong
And isn't your life extremely flat
With nothing whatever to grumble at!

— W. S. GILBERT

Nothing will content him who is not content with a little.

— GREEK PROVERB

All fortune belongs to him who has a contented mind. Is not
the whole earth covered with leather for him whose feet
are encased in shoes?

— PANCHATANTRA

If thou covetest riches, ask not but for contentment, which is
an immense treasure.

— SA'DI

The utmost we can hope for in this world is contentment; if
we aim at anything higher, we shall meet with nothing
but grief and disappointment.

— JOSEPH ADDISON

Good friends, good books, and a sleepy conscience: this is the
    ideal life.
                 — MARK TWAIN

My crown is in my heart, not on my head;
Not deck'd with diamonds and Indian stones,
Nor to be seen: my crown is called content;
A crown it is that seldom kings enjoy.
                 — WILLIAM SHAKESPEARE

When we cannot find contentment in ourselves it is useless to
    seek it elsewhere.
                 — LA ROCHEFOUCAULD

He may well be contented who needs neither borrow nor flatter.
                 — JOHN RAY

Happy the man, of mortals happiest he,
Whose quiet mind from vain desires is free;
Whom neither hopes deceive, nor fears torment,
But lives at peace, within himself content.
                 — GEORGE GRANVILLE

Content makes poor men rich; discontent makes rich men poor.
                 — BENJAMIN FRANKLIN

The secret of contentment is the realization that life is a gift, not a right.
— ANONYMOUS

You can't have everything. Where would you put it?
— STEVEN WRIGHT

Notwithstanding the poverty of my outside experience, I have always had a significance for myself, and every chance to stumble along my straight and narrow little path, and to worship at the feet of my Deity, and what more can a human soul ask for?
— ALICE JAMES

There are nine requisites for contented living: health enough to make work a pleasure; wealth enough to support your needs; strength to battle with difficulties and overcome them; grace enough to confess your sins and forsake them; patience enough to toil until some good is accomplished; charity enough to see some good in your neighbor; love enough to move you to be useful and helpful to others; faith enough to make real the things of God; hope enough to remove all anxious fears concerning the future.
— JOHANN WOLFGANG VON GOETHE

forgiveness

To err is human, to forgive divine.
> — ALEXANDER POPE

Forgiving presupposes remembering.
> — PAUL TILLICH

In taking revenge a man is but even with his enemy, but in passing it over he is superior, for it is a prince's part to pardon.
> — FRANCIS BACON

The truest joys they seldom prove,
    Who free from quarrels live;
'Tis the most tender part of love,
    Each other to forgive.
> — JOHN SHEFFIELD

A wise man will make haste to forgive, because he knows the true value of time, and will not suffer it to pass away in unnecessary pain.
> — SAMUEL JOHNSON

forgive others often, but yourself never.
— LATIN PROVERB

Once a woman has forgiven her man, she must not reheat his
sins for breakfast.
— MARLENE DIETRICH

The stupid neither forgive nor forget;
The naive forgive and forget;
The wise forgive but do not forget.
— THOMAS SZASZ

If you haven't forgiven yourself something, how can you forgive others?
— DOLORES HUERTA

If you understand something, you don't forgive it, you are the
thing itself: forgiveness is for what you *don't* understand.
— DORIS LESSING

Don't carry a grudge. While you're carrying the grudge, the
other guy's out dancing.
— BUDDY HACKETT

I think one should forgive and remember. . . . If you forgive
and forget in the usual sense, you're just driving what
you remember into the subconscious; it stays there and
festers. But to look, even regularly, upon what you
remember and *know* you've forgiven is achievement.
— FAITH BALDWIN

Children begin by loving their parents; as they grow older
they judge them; sometimes they forgive them.
— OSCAR WILDE

We must develop and maintain the capacity to forgive. He
who is devoid of the power to forgive is devoid of the
power to love. There is some good in the worst of us and
some evil in the best of us. When we discover this, we are
less prone to hate our enemies.
— MARTIN LUTHER KING JR.

He that cannot forgive others breaks the bridge over which he
must pass himself; for every man has need to be
forgiven.
— THOMAS FULLER, M.D.

For my part, I believe in the forgiveness of sin and the
redemption of ignorance.
— ADLAI E. STEVENSON

The weak can never forgive. Forgiveness is the attribute of
the strong.
—MAHATMA GANDHI

Always forgive your enemies; nothing annoys them so much.
—OSCAR WILDE

Forgiveness is the fragrance the violet sheds on the heel that
has crushed it.
—ANONYMOUS

gratitude

Some people are always grumbling because roses have thorns.
I am thankful that thorns have roses.
—ALPHONSE KARR

The sign outside the gates of salvation says, 'Be grateful.'
—MICHAEL LEVINE

Every time I fill a vacant office, I make ten malcontents and
one ingrate.
—LOUIS XIV

Into the well which supplies thee with water, cast no stones.
— TALMUD

It is a dangerous thing to ask why someone else has been given more. It is humbling—and indeed healthy—to ask why you have been given so much.
— CONDOLEEZZA RICE

A thankful heart is the parent of all virtues.
— CICERO

Let us give thanks for this beautiful day. Let us give thanks for this life. Let us give thanks for the water without which life would not be possible. Let us give thanks for Grandmother Earth who protects and nourishes us.
— DAILY PRAYER OF THE
LAKOTA AMERICAN INDIAN

When eating bamboo sprouts, remember the man who planted them.
— CHINESE PROVERB

When befriended, remember it; when you befriend, forget it.
— BENJAMIN FRANKLIN

Let me say that the credit belongs to the boys in the back rooms. It isn't the man who sits in the limelight like me who should have the praise. It is not the men who sit in prominent places. It is the men in the back rooms.
— LORD BEAVERBROOK

Wise men appreciate all men, for they see the good in each and know how hard it is to make anything good. ·
— BALTASAR GRACIÁN

I would rather be able to appreciate things I can not have than to have things I am not able to appreciate.
— ELBERT HUBBARD

No duty is more urgent than that of returning thanks.
— SAINT AMBROSE

If a fellow isn't thankful for what he's got, he isn't likely to be thankful for what he's going to get.
— FRANK A. CLARK

Gratitude is the heart's memory.
— FRENCH PROVERB

Humor

Men will let you abuse them if only you will make them
laugh.
— Henry Ward Beecher

A sense of humor keen enough to show a man his own absur-
dities, as well as those of other people, will keep him
from the commission of all sins, or nearly all, save those
that are worth committing.
— Samuel Butler

As brevity is the soul of wit, form, it seems to me, is the heart
of humor and the salvation of comedy.
— James Thurber

Men will confess to treason, murder, arson, false teeth, or a
wig. How many of them will own up to a lack of humor?
— Frank Moore Colby

A difference of taste in jokes is a great strain on the affections.
— George Eliot

Humor simultaneously wounds and heals, indicts and pardons, diminishes and enlarges; it constitutes inner growth at the expense of outer gain, and those who possess and honestly practice it make themselves more through a willingness to make themselves less.

— LOUIS KRONENBERGER

Wit has truth in it; wisecracking is simply calisthenics with words.

— DOROTHY PARKER

Closely related to faith; [humor] bids us not to take anything too seriously.

— FULTON J. SHEEN

It's hard to be funny when you have to be clean.

— MAE WEST

Humor is a serious thing. I like to think of it as one of our greatest and earliest national resources which must be preserved at all costs.

— JAMES THURBER

serenity

There is no joy but calm.
> — ALFRED, LORD TENNYSON

As a rule, for no one does life drag more disagreeably than for
him who tries to speed it up.
> — JOHANN PAUL FRIEDRICH
> RICHTER

Do not let trifles disturb your tranquillity of mind. . . . Life is
too precious to be sacrificed for the nonessential and
transient. . . . Ignore the inconsequential.
> — GRENVILLE KLEISER

I have laid aside business, and gone a-fishing.
> — IZAAK WALTON

Do not seek to have everything that happens happen as you
wish, but wish for everything to happen as it actually
does happen, and your life will be serene.
> — EPICTETUS

The world is not to be put in order, the world is in order. It is
for us to put ourselves in unison with this order.
— HENRY MILLER

Were all the year one constant sunshine, we
    Should have no flowers,
All would be draught and leanness; not a tree
    Would make us bowers;
Beauty consists in colors; and that's best
Which is not fixed, but flies and flowers.
— HENRY VAUGHAN

In the depth of winter, I finally learned that within me there
lay an invincible summer.
— ALBERT CAMUS

Happiness

Happiness depends upon ourselves.
— ARISTOTLE

The bird of paradise alights only upon the hand that does not
grasp.
— JOHN BERRY

He that is of a merry heart hath a continual feast.
—PROVERBS 15:15

One moment may with bliss repay
Unnumbered hours of pain.
—THOMAS CAMPBELL

Happiness is not best achieved by those who seek it directly.
—BERTRAND RUSSELL

Happiness, that grand mistress of the ceremonies in the dance
of life, impels us through all its mazes and meanderings,
but leads none of us by the same route.
—CHARLES CALEB COLTON

True joy is the nearest which we have of heaven, it is the treasure of the soul, and therefore should be laid in a safe
place, and nothing in this world is safe to place it in.
—JOHN DONNE

Human felicity is produced not so much by great pieces of
good fortune that seldom happen as by little advantages
that occur every day.
—BENJAMIN FRANKLIN

Happiness makes up in height for what it lacks in length.
— ROBERT FROST

When one door of happiness closes, another opens; but often
    we look so long at the closed door that we do not see the
    one which has been opened for us.
— HELEN KELLER

Happiness is itself a kind of gratitude.
— JOSEPH WOOD KRUTCH

When you jump for joy, beware that no one moves the
    ground from beneath your feet.
— STANISLAW LEC

I am happy and content because I think I am.
— ALAIN-RÉNÉ LESAGE

There are many roads
to happiness, if the gods assent.
— PINDAR

No man is happy who does not think himself so.
— PUBLILIUS SYRUS

Most people ask for happiness on condition. Happiness can
only be felt if you don't set any condition.
— ARTHUR RUBINSTEIN

Man needs, for his happiness, not only the enjoyment of this
or that, but hope and enterprise and change.
— BERTRAND RUSSELL

I find my joy of living in the fierce and ruthless battles of life,
and my pleasure comes from learning something.
— AUGUST STRINDBERG

The trouble is not that we are never happy—it is that
happiness is so episodical.
— RUTH BENEDICT

Happiness? A good cigar, a good meal, a good cigar and a
good woman—or a bad woman; it depends on how
much happiness you can handle.
— GEORGE BURNS

That is happiness; to be dissolved into something complete
and great.
— WILLA CATHER

People need joy quite as much as clothing. Some of them
need it far more.
— MARGARET COLLIER GRAHAM

Happiness is a habit—cultivate it.
— ELBERT HUBBARD

How to gain, how to keep, how to recover happiness is in fact
for most men at all times the secret motive of all they do,
and of all they are willing to endure.
— WILLIAM JAMES

Kissing your hand may make you feel very, very good but a
diamond and sapphire bracelet lasts forever.
— ANITA LOOS

Puritanism—the haunting fear that someone, somewhere,
may be happy.
— H. L. MENCKEN

Where's the man could ease a heart
Like a satin gown?
— DOROTHY PARKER

Happiness is a way station between too little and too much.
— CHANNING POLLOCK

Modern Americans travel light, with little philosophic baggage other than a fervent belief in their right to the pursuit of happiness.
— GEORGE WILL

My life has no purpose, no direction, no aim, no meaning, and
yet I'm happy. I can't figure it out. What am I doing
right?
— CHARLES SCHULZ

The secret of happiness is this: Let your interests be as wide as
possible, and let your reactions to the things and persons
that interest you be as far as possible friendly rather than
hostile.
— BERTRAND RUSSELL

The happy man is not he who seems thus to others, but who
seems thus to himself.
— PUBLILIUS SYRUS

Happiness is not a state to arrive at, but a manner of traveling.
— MARGARET LEE RUNBECK

There is nothing which has yet been contrived by man by which so much happiness is produced as by a good tavern.
—SAMUEL JOHNSON

If happiness truly consisted in physical ease and freedom from care, then the happiest individual would not be either a man or a woman; it would be, I think, an American cow.
—WILLIAM LYON PHELPS

The happiest man is he who learns from nature the lesson of worship.
—RALPH WALDO EMERSON

If a man has important work, and enough leisure and income to enable him to do it properly, he is in possession of as much happiness as is good for any of the children of Adam.
—R. H. TAWNEY

What a wonderful life I've had! I only wish I'd realized it sooner.
—COLETTE

Joy is not in things; it is in us.
—RICHARD WAGNER

It is the chiefest point of happiness that a man is willing to be
what he is.
— ERASMUS

If you ever find happiness by hunting for it, you will find it,
as the old woman did her lost spectacles, safe on her own
nose all the time.
— JOSH BILLINGS

Whoever is happy will make others happy too.
— ANNE FRANK

To be happy, we must not be too concerned with others.
— ALBERT CAMUS

Happiness is mostly a by-product of doing what makes us feel
fulfilled.
— BENJAMIN SPOCK

If only we'd stop trying to be happy, we could have a pretty
good time.
— EDITH WHARTON

Happiness is equilibrium. Shift your weight. Equilibrium is
    pragmatic. You have to get everything into proportion.
    You compensate, rebalance yourself so that you maintain
    your angle to your world. When the world shifts, you
    shift.
                            — TOM STOPPARD

More and more it seems the faithful distort God's message
    and hear, 'Love thy neighbor, hate thyself.'
                            — MICHAEL LEVINE

Compare what you want with what you have, and you'll be
    unhappy; compare what you deserve with what you
    have, and you'll be happy.
                            — EVAN ESAR

Talk happiness. The world is sad enough
Without your woe. No path is wholly rough.
                            — ELLA WHEELER WILCOX

Every time I talk to a savant I feel quite sure that happiness is
    no longer a possibility. Yet when I talk with my gardener,
    I'm convinced of the opposite.
                            — BERTRAND RUSSELL

Your best shot at happiness, self-worth, and personal satisfaction—the things that constitute real success—is not in earning as much as you can but in performing as well as you can something that you consider worthwhile. Whether that is healing the sick, giving hope to the hopeless, adding to the beauty of the world, or saving the world from nuclear holocaust, I cannot tell you.
— WILLIAM RASPBERRY

Happiness is like a cat. If you try to coax it or call it, it will avoid you. It will never come. But if you pay no attention to it and go about your business, you'll find it rubbing against your legs and jumping into your lap. So forget pursuing happiness. Pin your hopes on work, on family, on learning, on knowing, on loving. Forget pursuing happiness, pursue these other things, and with luck happiness will come.
— WILLIAM BENNETT

No matter how dull, or how mean, or how wise a man is, he feels that happiness is his indisputable right.
— HELEN KELLER

The best way to secure future happiness is to be as happy as is rightfully possible today.
— CHARLES W. ELIOT

We find a delight in the beauty and happiness of children,
that makes the heart too big for the body.
— RALPH WALDO EMERSON

I care not much for gold or land;—
    Give me a mortgage here and there,—
Some good bank-stock, some note of hand,
    Or trifling railroad share,—
I only ask that Fortune send
A *little* more than I shall spend.
— OLIVER WENDELL HOLMES SR.

What wisdom, what warning can prevail against gladness?
    There is no law so strong which a little gladness may not
    transgress.
— HENRY DAVID THOREAU

Grief can take care of itself, but to get the full value of a joy
    you must have somebody to divide it with.
— MARK TWAIN

Happiness must be cultivated. It is like character. It is not a
    thing to be safely let alone for a moment, or it will run to
    weeds.
— ELIZABETH STUART PHELPS

The U.S. Constitution doesn't guarantee happiness, only the pursuit of it. You have to catch up to it yourself.
— BENJAMIN FRANKLIN

You have to sniff out joy, keep your nose to the joy-trail.
— BUFFY SAINTE-MARIE

It is not easy to find happiness in ourselves, and it is impossible to find it elsewhere.
— AGNES REPPLIER

The happiest people seem to be those who have no particular reason for being happy except that they are so.
— DEAN WILLIAM R. INGE

Happiness is a how, not a what; talent, not an object.
— HERMANN HESSE

Anyone who thinks money will make you happy doesn't have money. Happiness is more difficult to obtain than money.
— DAVID GEFFEN

PART II

COURAGE

Most Americans I have met think that courage is the absence of fear. Yet several of the following quotes take pains to point out that it is not; courage is the capacity to go ahead in spite of your fear—in the very direction of which you are afraid. In fact, as far as I am concerned, the total absence of fear suggests some kind of brain damage.

Sometime in my early, preconscious childhood I made a trade-off. I became a physical coward. I was the last of my peers to swim out to the float because of my fear of drowning. I was late in learning how to ride a bike. When other kids tried to fight me, I just curled up in a ball. When I finally learned to ski I was the safest skier in the world; I wouldn't even risk falling down. I may even have become a physician in order to avoid ever having to go through basic training in the military. By early adulthood my distinct self-image was that of a "chicken."

So it was initially a considerable surprise to me when many of my readers wrote to praise me for my courage. The most common response to my books has been not that I have written anything completely new, but that in them I said things that the readers already thought but were afraid to talk about—things that caused them to fear for their sanity or, at least, the disapprobation of their friends. Perhaps I wasn't a total coward after all. Perhaps I had somehow traded off physical courage in favor of intellectual courage.

I am today rather pleased by that trade-off. I do not mean to decry physical courage. Often it is mindless, but when it is not, it is indeed a great virtue, although thus far one I seem to lack. I very much admire Christa McAuliffe for flying off into space even though it was to meet her death. Hers was not a senseless death, and I hope for the courage to decently meet my own . . . albeit, hopefully, from natural causes. Nonetheless, as I look at my nation, I am generally impressed by the physical courage of its citizenry but distressed by the lack of intellectual or moral courage. I think this is important because most quotes about bravery refer to physical courage. Yet if my nation is to go down the tubes, I suspect it will be more because of a deficit in its intellectual bravery.

Sally Ride, the first female astronaut, has said: "All adventures, especially into new territory, are scary." It is simply human to be afraid of going into the unknown. Indeed, it is wise. But it is also only from adventures that we learn. If you know exactly where you're going, exactly how you're going to get there, and exactly what you'll see along the way, it's hardly an adventure. It is also not very likely that you'll learn anything from the experience. I believe the point is even more true for intellectual than for physical adventures. Certainly I have been deeply enriched by all the extraordinary things I have seen along the way of my intellectual meanderings. It's been an exciting journey.

But what was the origin of my strange intellectual adventurousness? I do not know. As with so many matters, I imagine there was more than one cause. The one I am most certain about occurred in early childhood after my parents had caught me lying in the attempt to cover up a mistake I'd made. "Face the music," they instructed me. That intriguing proverb you will shortly find paraphrased by an intellectual adventurer far greater than I, T. S. Eliot, when he said, "Whatever you do . . . don't whimper, but take the consequences."

Most lying can be traced to the fear of taking the consequences of one's actions. Conversely it takes courage to face the music. What I am saying here is that most truth telling is courageous, and most lying an act of cowardice. At the risk of being repetitive, please remember that all the virtues are interconnected and interdependent. Part VIII of this book is about the multiple component virtues of goodness. Of those virtues I believe the most important is truthfulness. When we come to it, you will be reading more about the permutations of courage.

I am grateful to my parents for urging me to face the music. But why did I decide to take them up on it? Here we get into the mysterious realm of virtues as gifts (touched upon in the introduction). I am reminded of the movie *Chariots of Fire*. One of its two central characters is a Scottish Christian man, a greatly gifted Olympic runner of both extraordinary intellectual as well as physical courage (he was ultimately to be killed as a missionary martyr). At one point in the film his sister demanded to know how he could run in a seemingly unChristian competition. He answered her simply, by explaining, "God made me fast."

Bravery

I have done one braver thing
    Than all the worthies did;
And yet a braver thing doth spring,
    Which is, to keep that hid.
            — JOHN DONNE

Familiarity with danger makes a brave man braver, but less
    daring. Thus with seamen: he who goes the oftenest
    round Cape Horn goes the most circumspectly.
            — HERMAN MELVILLE

If you're scared, just holler and you'll find it ain't so lonesome
    out there.
            — JOE SUGDEN

The better part of valor is discretion.
            — WILLIAM SHAKESPEARE

Valor is a gift. Those having it never know for sure whether
    they have it till the test comes. And those having it in one
    test never know for sure if they will have it when the
    next test comes.
            — CARL SANDBURG

Perfect valor is to do without witnesses what one would do
before all the world.
— La Rochefoucauld

Bravery is the capacity to perform properly even when scared
half to death.
— General Omar Bradley

This will remain the land of the free only so long as it is the
home of the brave.
— Elmer Davis

Valor and boastfulness never buckle on the same sword.
— Japanese proverb

When valor preys on reason, it eats the sword it fights with.
— William Shakespeare

True valor lies in the middle, between cowardice and rashness.
— Cervantes

If men were just, there would be no need of valor.
— Agesilaus

fortitude

fortitude is the marshal of thought, the armor of the will, and
the fort of the reason.
— FRANCIS BACON

Bite on the bullet, old man, and don't let them think you're
afraid.
— RUDYARD KIPLING

I don't need a man to rectify my existence. The most profound
relationship we'll ever have is the one with ourselves.
— SHIRLEY MACLAINE

Bear, do not blame, what cannot be changed.
— PUBLILIUS SYRUS

You gotta play the hand that's dealt you. There may be pain in
that hand, but you play it. And I've played it.
— JAMES BRADY

Whatever you do ... don't whimper, but take the consequences.
— T. S. ELIOT

I still dream big at times, but when my dreams pull apart, as they sometimes do, I don't press the panic button.
— GORDON PARKS

How wrong it is for woman to expect the man to build the world she wants, rather than set out to create it herself.
— ANAÏS NIN

The proverb warns that, "You should not bite the hand that feeds you." But maybe you should, if it prevents you from feeding yourself.
— THOMAS SZASZ

The wishbone will never replace the backbone.
— WILL HENRY

courage

Courage is the thing. All goes if courage goes.
— J. M. BARRIE

Until the day of his death, no man can be sure of his courage.
— JEAN ANOUILH

Courage is resistance to fear, mastery of fear—not absence of fear. Except a creature be part coward it is not a compliment to say it is brave.
— MARK TWAIN

Do not follow where the path may lead. Go instead where there is no path and leave a trail.
— MURIEL STRODE

Courage is fear that has said its prayers.
— DOROTHY BERNARD

You gain strength, courage and confidence by every experience in which you really stop to look fear in the face. . . . You must do the thing which you think you cannot do.
— ELEANOR ROOSEVELT

No one can answer for his courage when he has never been in danger.
— LA ROCHEFOUCAULD

Courage is worth nothing if the gods withhold their aid.
— EURIPIDES

Courage is the price that life exacts for granting peace. The soul that knows it not, knows no release from little things; knows not the livid loneliness of fear.
— AMELIA EARHART

Courage is like love; it must have hope for nourishment.
— NAPOLEON I

Sometimes even to live is an act of courage.
— SENECA

Often the test of courage is not to die but to live.
— VITTORIO ALFIERI

What is to give light must endure burning.
— VIKTOR FRANKL

The courage of the tiger is one, and of the horse another.
— RALPH WALDO EMERSON

To gain that which is worth having, it may be necessary to lose everything.
— BERNADETTE DEVLIN

Courage without conscience is a wild beast.
— R. G. INGERSOLL

You can't be brave if you've only had wonderful things happen to you.
— MARY TYLER MOORE

Life shrinks or expands in proportion to one's courage.
— ANAÏS NIN

All adventures, especially into new territory, are scary.
— SALLY RIDE

It is from numberless diverse acts of courage and belief that human history is shaped. Each time a man stands up for an ideal or acts to improve the lot of others or strikes out against injustice, he sends forth a tiny ripple of hope, and crossing each other from a million different centers of energy and daring those ripples build a current which can sweep down the mightiest walls of oppression and resistance.
— ROBERT F. KENNEDY

Courage is the ladder on which all the other virtues mount.
— CLARE BOOTH LUCE

There is nothing to fear except the persistent refusal to find
out the truth, the persistent refusal to analyze the causes
of happenings. Fear grows in darkness; if you think
there's a bogeyman around, turn on the light.
— DOROTHY THOMPSON

He serves all who dares be true.
— RALPH WALDO EMERSON

The Ancient Mariner said to Neptune during a great storm,
"O God, you will save me if you wish, but I am going to
go on holding my tiller straight."
— MICHEL DE MONTAIGNE

Courage, the footstool of the Virtues, upon which they stand.
— ROBERT LOUIS STEVENSON

If Rosa Parks had not refused to move to the back of the bus,
you and I might never have heard of Dr. Martin Luther
King.
— RAMSEY CLARK

Courage is almost a contradiction in terms. It means a strong
desire to live taking the form of a readiness to die.
— G. K. CHESTERTON

To laugh is to risk appearing the fool.

To weep is to risk appearing sentimental.

To reach for another is to risk involvement.

To expose your feelings is to risk exposing your true self.

To place your ideas, your dreams before a crowd is to risk
their loss.

To love is to risk not being loved in return.

To live is to risk dying.

To believe is to risk despair.

To try is to risk failure.

But risks must be taken, because the greatest hazard in life is
to risk nothing.

The person who risks nothing, does nothing, has nothing, is
nothing.

They may avoid suffering and sorrow, but they cannot learn,
feel, change, grow, love, live.

Chained by their attitudes they are slaves; they have forfeited
their freedom.

Only a person who risks is free.

— ANONYMOUS CHICAGO TEACHER

I'd feel a lot braver if I wasn't so scared.

— HAWKEYE PIERCE, *M*A*S*H*

He was a bold man who first swallowed an oyster.

— JAMES I

If God wanted us to be brave, why did He give us legs?
— Marvin Kitman

Courage is doing what you're afraid to do. There can be no
courage unless you're scared.
— Eddie Rickenbacker

None but a coward dares to boast that he has never known fear.
— Marshal Ferdinand Foch

It often takes more courage to change one's opinion than to
stick to it.
— George Christoph Lictenberg

One thinks like a hero to behave like a merely decent human
being.
— May Sarton

What counts is not necessarily the size of the dog in the
fight—it's the size of the fight in the dog.
— Dwight D. Eisenhower

Bravery is being the only one who knows you're afraid.
— Franklin P. Jones

Never let your head hang down. Never give up and sit down
and grieve. Find another way. And don't pray when it
rains if you don't pray when the sun shines.
— SATCHEL PAIGE

We must face what we fear; that is the case of the core of the
restoration of health.
— MAX LERNER

The courage of life is often a less dramatic spectacle than the
courage of a final moment; but it is no less a magnificent
mixture of triumph and tragedy. A man does what he
must—in spite of personal consequences, in spite of
obstacles and dangers and pressures—and that is the
basis of all morality.
— JOHN F. KENNEDY

One doesn't discover new lands without consenting to lose
sight of the shore for a very long time.
— ANDRÉ GIDE

A great part of courage is the courage of having done the
thing before.
— RALPH WALDO EMERSON

The bravest thing you can do when you are not brave is to profess courage and act accordingly.
— CORRA HARRIS

The nation had the lion's heart. I had the luck to give the roar.
— WINSTON CHURCHILL

Adventures are to the adventurous.
— BENJAMIN DISRAELI

It is an error to suppose that courage means courage in everything.
— EDWARD BULWER-LYTTON

The probability that we may fail in the struggle ought not to deter us from the support of a cause we believe to be just.
— ABRAHAM LINCOLN

If one is forever cautious, can one remain a human being?
— ALEKSANDR SOLZHENITSYN

When moral courage feels that it is in the right, there is no personal daring of which it is incapable.
— LEIGH HUNT

The question is not whether you're frightened or not, but whether you or the fear is in control. If you say, "I won't be frightened," and then you experience fear, most likely you'll succumb to it, because you're paying attention to it. The correct thing to tell yourself is, "If I do get frightened, I will stay in command."
— DR. HERBERT FENSTERHEIM

So what if they're taller? We'll play big!
— COACH GEORGE IRELAND

Behold the turtle. He makes progress only when he sticks his neck out.
— JAMES B. CONANT

Why not go out on a limb? Isn't that where the fruit is?
— FRANK SCULLY

Last, but by no means least, courage—moral courage, the courage of one's convictions, the courage to see things through. The world is in a constant conspiracy against the brave. It's the age-old struggle—the roar of the crowd on one side and the voice of your conscience on the other.
— GENERAL DOUGLAS MACARTHUR

PART III

COMPASSION

Compassion and its component virtues, such as charity and generosity, are complex. I know.

In 1984 when we began to make more money than we cared to spend or even save, my wife, Lily, and I participated in the establishment of a charitable foundation, the Foundation for Community Encouragement, or FCE. Other than marriage and parenthood, our work with FCE has been the greatest adventure and hence the greatest learning experience of our lives. The learning has not always been easy or pleasant.

One thing we learned quite quickly was that by giving away large sums to FCE we were actually encouraging a dependency mentality on the part of many of its employees. Instead of doing their own work of fund-raising, an attitude rapidly came to prevail that "the Pecks will provide"—as if we were a bottomless pit. We had to work long and hard, confrontationally more than kindly, before the organization was healed of that attitude. Julius Rosenwald, the entrepreneurial genius behind Sears, Roebuck and founder of the Julius Rosenwald Fund, summed it up correctly when he declared, "It is almost always easier to make a million dollars honestly than to dispose of it wisely."

Sometimes reality is harsh. Some years ago I read the proceedings of a conference of community builders held in Nova Scotia. One of the speakers—a man who had been sacrificially on the front lines for two decades—said, "The most important thing we can do for the poor is to not become one of them." Does that sound callous? But consider the fact that FCE has been able to continue its community building work around the globe—some of which has been antipoverty work—only because it has continued to have a little money in the till and somehow managed to balance its books.

What I have been saying is a manifestation of that old saw, "Charity begins at home." What we usually take this to mean is that your first responsibility is to your family. And so it is . . . externally. But it is actually a more radical matter than that. Your first responsibility is to yourself. You cannot give away money you do not have. You will only create confusion if you attempt to love others when you don't love yourself. Indeed, the most crucial variety of compassion is self-compassion.

I have briefly focused upon money because it is the most tangible example of the ambiguities of charity, generosity, and the expression of compassion. But other examples abound. Keeping things at home, for the moment, consider the complexity of the decisions parents need to make if they're going to be wisely compassionate in their role of child raising. It is not just a matter of when you give your child an allowance or how much. For instance, if you catch your child in a minor lie, when do you confront her on it and when do you let her get away with it? If you yourself are feeling almost stretched to the limit, when do you walk an extra mile and take him to the skating rink or when do you tell him to amuse himself? What is the proper time for "tough love" as opposed to "soft love"?

There are no formalistic answers to such dilemmas of parenthood. I have but one hint. If there was any single blessing I could bestow upon parents it would be the ability to remember what it was like when they themselves were children. Childhood is not an easy time, and we adults often tend to forget that.

Although "charity always begins at home," it hardly ends

there. The opportunities to demonstrate compassion are, in fact, endless. They are in the workplace, the marketplace, and on the street. Presuming that you have an obligation to yourself to preserve at least some of your time and energy, whendo you make the effort to remark to a coworker, "It looks like you're having a bad day?" And make the space to really listen to his answer? The same would apply to the woman at the check-out lane of the supermarket you'll go to this weekend. And what if you should happen to run across a person begging in the street?

The quotes that follow generally succeed in capturing these sorts of ambiguities and complexities in regard to the matter of compassion. Yet some of them would strike me as unrealistic and almost sickeningly sweet were it not for the fact that I have some slight familiarity with the *mystery* of compassion. Nobody taught me better about that mystery than Charlie.

Charlie was a tough businessman and a member of one of the early community building workshops I led (work that is now done by FCE). He was the first member to speak. "I sense that most of you here are do-gooder liberals," he said. "I just want to let you know up front that I'm a Republican and you're probably going to hate my guts."

Thereafter Charlie did not speak until close to the end of that two-day workshop. Let me conclude by quoting him in his own words, as best as I can remember them:

I don't know why I feel compelled to tell you this story, but I do. Anyway, about two years ago I was walking down the street of the suburb where we live when I was accosted by a panhandler.

He was obviously a severe alcoholic. His red face was unshaven for a week and his pants still wet with urine. Ordinarily I would have passed him by. However, I had just received a small, unexpected inheritance. I also regarded myself as a Christian, and it seemed incumbent upon me to give him *something*. Yet I knew that if I gave him money he'd just spend it on more booze—the last thing I thought he needed. But I imagined he did need food. It so happened we were standing right in front of a McDonald's. I told him I'd take him in and buy him a hamburger. He hardly seemed enthusiastic but he did follow me.

I bought him a Big Mac and sat with him while he reluctantly ate half of it, which seemed to be all he could stomach. I don't remember us talking, but I guess I must at least have told him my name. When we emerged I felt unhappy—certainly a failure as a do-gooder. And that was when the damnedest thing happened. I can't explain it.

Anyway, I knew there was a liquor store right around the corner. It was like I became somebody else. I took his elbow, walked him into the liquor store, bought a fifth of bourbon, and gave it to him. He looked pleased, but I didn't give a damn. If anything, I felt bad because I'd done the wrong thing, and I left him there still standing in the store.

That's it, I guess, except for one more piece that's probably unrelated. A couple of months later I was walking down the street again when a bus passed by. A man leaned his head out of the window. He was clean-shaven, and at first I didn't recognize him. But as the bus roared past I could swear I heard him yell at me, "Hey, Charlie, I've been dry for two weeks now!"

charity

Charity begins at home, but should not end there.
— THOMAS FULLER, M.D.

The charitable give out at the door, and God puts in at the window.
— JOHN RAY

We should be strengthening the hand of the poor rather than simply putting something into it.
— WIL ROSE

I as little fear that God will damn a man that has charity, as I hope that the priests can save one who has not.
— ALEXANDER POPE

Though I have all faith, so that I could remove mountains, and have not charity, I am nothing.
— I CORINTHIANS 13:2

Charity, to be fruitful, must cost us.
— MOTHER TERESA

We cannot exist without mutual help. All, therefore, that
need aid have a right to ask it from their fellow men, and
no one who has the power of granting can refuse it without guilt.
— SIR WALTER SCOTT

The robbed that smiles steals something from the thief.
— WILLIAM SHAKESPEARE

A man may bestow great sums on the poor and indigent without being charitable, and may be charitable when he is
not able to bestow anything.
— JOSEPH ADDISON

There is an ordinary proverb for this: "Stinginess does not
enrich; charity does not impoverish."
— GLUCKEL OF HAMELIN

The law of mutual charity perfects the law of justice.
— POPE LEO XIII

No one would remember the Good Samaritan if he'd only
had good intentions. He had money as well.
— MARGARET THATCHER

Posthumous charities are the very essence of selfishness when bequeathed by those who, when alive, would part with nothing.
— CHARLES CALEB COLTON

For it is to the humanity in a man that we give, and not to his moral character.
— JULIAN THE APOSTATE

At the Harvest Festival in church the area behind the pulpit was piled high with tins of fruit for the old-age pensioners. We had collected the tinned fruit from door to door. Most of it came from old-age pensioners.
— CLIVE JAMES

There are eight rungs in charity. The highest is when you help a man to help himself.
— MOSES MAIMONIDES

Scatter abroad what you have already amassed rather than pile up new wealth.
— 'ALI

If you want to lift yourself up, lift up someone else.
— BOOKER T. WASHINGTON

Bread for myself is a material question; bread for my neighbor is a spiritual question.
— JACQUES MARITAIN

The eight grades of charity:
1. to give reluctantly
2. to give cheerfully but not adequately
3. to give cheerfully and adequately, but only after being asked
4. to give cheerfully, adequately, and of your own free will, but to put it in the recipient's hand in such a way as to make him feel lesser
5. to let the recipient know who the donor is, but not the reverse
6. to know who is receiving your charity but to remain anonymous to him
7. to have neither the donor nor the recipient be aware of the other's identity
8. to dispense with charity altogether, by enabling your fellow humans to have the wherewithal to earn their own living
— MOSES MAIMONIDES

The trick of living is to slip on and off the planet with the least fuss you can muster. I'm not a professional philanthropist, and I'm not running for sainthood. I just happen to think that in life we need to be a little like the farmer who puts back into the soil what he takes out.
— PAUL NEWMAN

Don't use the impudence of a beggar as an excuse for not
helping him.
— RABBI SCHMELKE OF NICOLSBURG

Giving is the secret of a healthy life. Not necessarily money,
but whatever a man has of encouragement and sympathy
and understanding.
— JOHN D. ROCKEFELLER JR.

You do not have to be rich to be generous. If he has the spirit
of true generosity, a pauper can give like a prince.
— CORRINE U. WELLS

generosity

We should give as we would receive, cheerfully, quickly, and
without hesitation; for there is no grace in a benefit that
sticks to the fingers.
— SENECA

People who think they're generous to a fault usually think
that's their only fault.
— SYDNEY J. HARRIS

He's so generous, he'd give you the sleeves out of his vest.
— ANONYMOUS

Generosity gives assistance, rather than advice.
— VAUVENARGUES

Giving is the highest expression of potency.
— ERICH FROMM

If you have much, give of your wealth; if you have little, give
of your heart.
— ARAB PROVERB

Leave the field, thou art victorious; it is noble to spare the
vanquished.
— STATIUS

Feel for others—in your pocket.
— C. H. SPURGEON

In War: Resolution. In Defeat: Defiance.
In Victory: Magnanimity. In Peace: Good Will.
— WINSTON CHURCHILL

Hospitality

A guest never forgets the host who had treated him kindly.
— HOMER

Be not forgetful to entertain strangers, for thereby some have entertained angels unawares.
— HEBREWS 13:1–2

For I was an hungered, and ye gave me meat: I was thirsty, and ye gave me drink: I was a stranger, and ye took me in.
— MATTHEW 25:35

When there is room in the heart, there is room in the house.
— DANISH PROVERB

Come again when you can't stay so long.
— WALTER SICKERT

To revolutionize a whole house on the coming of a few visitors betrays not only poor taste, but an absolute lack of character. Let your friends come into your life; let them see you as you are, and not find you trying to be somebody else.
— EMMA WHITCOMB BABCOOK

kindness

The unfortunate need people who will be kind to them; the prosperous need people to be kind to.
— ARISTOTLE

I expect to pass through life but once. If therefore, there be any kindness I can show, or any good thing I can do to any fellow being, let me do it now, and not defer or neglect it, as I shall not pass this way again.
— WILLIAM PENN

The drying up a single tear has more
Of honest fame, than shedding seas of gore.
— GEORGE GORDON, LORD BYRON

Human kindness has never weakened the stamina or softened the fiber of a free people. A nation does not have to be cruel to be tough.
— FRANKLIN D. ROOSEVELT

We live very close together. So, our prime purpose in this life is to help others. And if you can't help them, at least don't hurt them.
— DALAI LAMA

A word of kindness is better than a fat pie.
— RUSSIAN PROVERB

One kind word can warm three Winter months.
— JAPANESE PROVERB

One who knows how to show and to accept kindness will be
a friend better than any possession.
— SOPHOCLES

That best portion of a good man's life,
His little, nameless, unremembered acts
Of kindness and of love.
— WILLIAM WORDSWORTH

Kindness in women, not their beauteous looks,
Shall win my love.
— WILLIAM SHAKESPEARE

Constant kindness can accomplish much. As the sun makes
ice melt, kindness causes misunderstanding, mistrust
and hostility to evaporate.
— ALBERT SCHWEITZER

True kindness presupposes the faculty of imagining as one's own the suffering and joys of others.
— ANDRÉ GIDE

A part of kindness consists in loving people more than they deserve.
— JOSEPH JOUBERT

In this world, you must be a bit too kind in order to be kind enough.
— PIERRE CARLET DE CHAMBLAIN DE MARIVAUX

Kindness is a language the deaf can hear and the dumb can understand.
— ANONYMOUS

When kindness has left people, even for a few moments, we become afraid of them as if their reason has left them.
— WILLA CATHER

He was so benevolent, so merciful a man that, in his mistaken passion, he would have held an umbrella over a duck in a shower of rain.
— DOUGLAS JERROLD

So many gods, so many creeds,
So many paths that wind and wind,
While just the art of being kind
Is all the sad world needs.
— ELLA WHEELER WILCOX

You can get more with a kind word and a gun than you can
get with a kind word alone.
— JOHNNY CARSON

Wise sayings often fall on barren ground; but a kind word is
never thrown away.
— SIR ARTHUR HELPS

Throw out the lifeline, throw out the lifeline,
Someone is sinking today.
— EDWARD SMITH UFFORD

Kindness has converted more sinners than zeal, eloquence, or
learning.
— FREDERICK W. FABER

One can pay back the loan of gold, but one lies forever in debt
to those who are kind.
— MARCUS AURELIUS

Do not feel badly if your kindness is rewarded with ingratitude; it is better to fall from your dream clouds than from a third-story window.
— JOAQUIM MARIA MACHADO DE ASSIS

A great man shows his greatness by the way he treats little men.
— THOMAS CARLYLE

What do we live for, if it is not to make life less difficult for each other?
— GEORGE ELIOT

Kindness begets kindness.
— SOPHOCLES

Never lose a chance of saying a kind word.
— WILLIAM MAKEPEACE THACKERAY

Paradise is open to all kind hearts.
— PIERRE JEAN DE BÉRANGER

Man is honored for his wisdom, loved for his kindness.
— S. COHEN

There are three rules of dealing with all those who come to
us: 1. Kindness; 2. Kindness; 3. Kindness.
— FULTON J. SHEEN

A little more kindness and a little less creed,
A little more giving and a little less greed;
A little more smile and a little less frown,
A little less kicking a man when he's down;
A little more "we" and a little less "I,"
A little more laugh and a little less cry;
A few more flowers on the pathway of life,
And fewer on graves at the end of the strife.
— ANONYMOUS

mercy

The quality of mercy is not strained;
It droppeth as the gentle rain from heaven
Upon the place beneath. It is twice blessed—
It blesseth him that gives, and him that takes.
— WILLIAM SHAKESPEARE

Have mercy upon me, O Lord; for I am weak:
O Lord, heal me; for my bones are vexed.
— PSALM 6:2

Less pleasure take brave minds in battles won,
Than in restoring such as are undone;
Tigers have courage, and the rugged bear,
But man alone can, whom he conquers, spare.
— EDMUND WALLER

Pour not water on a drowning mouse.
— THOMAS FULLER, M.D.

God tempers the wind to the shorn lamb.
— ENGLISH PROVERB

God be merciful unto us, and bless us; and cause his face to
shine upon us.
— PSALM 67:1

It is a bad cause that asks for mercy.
— PUBLILIUS SYRUS

Mercy imitates God and disappoints Satan.
— ST. JOHN CHRYSOSTOM

Who shows mercy to an enemy, denies it to himself.
— FRANCIS BACON

Mercies that are ordinary we swallow, and take small notice
of them.
— ANONYMOUS

The mercy of the Lord is from everlasting to everlasting upon
them that fear him.
— PSALM 103:17

In case of doubt it is best to lean to the side of mercy.
— LEGAL MAXIM

pity

If every man's internal care
Were written on his brow,
How many would our pity share,
Who raise our envy now!
— WILLIAM SAVAGE LANDOR

Youth feels pity out of human kindness; old age out of its
infirmity.
— ARISTOTLE

unselfishness

To gain that which is worth having, it may be necessary to
lose everything else.
— BERNADETTE D. McALISKEY

To reach perfection, we must all pass, one by one, through the
death of self-effacement.
— DAG HAMMARSKJÖLD

"I haven't got time to be sick!" he said. "People need me." For
he was a country doctor, and he did not know what it
was to spare himself.
— DON MARQUIS

Drown not thyself to save a drowning man.
— THOMAS FULLER, M.D.

for it is not possible that the blood of bulls and of goats should
take away sins.
— HEBREWS 10:4

We shall not lightly talk about sacrifice until we are driven to
the last extremity which makes sacrifice inevitable.
— CHIANG KAI-SHEK

If we ever get free from all the oppressions and wrongs heaped
upon us, we must pay for their removal. We must do this
by labor, by suffering, by sacrifice, and, if needs be, by our
lives, and the lives of others.
—FREDERICK DOUGLASS

The way to get things done is not to mind who gets the
credit of doing them.
—BENJAMIN JEWETT

The willing sacrifice of the innocents is the most powerful
retort to insolent tyranny that has yet to be conceived by
God or man.
—MAHATMA GANDHI

In this world it is not what we take up, but what we give up,
that makes us rich.
—HENRY WARD BEECHER

I may be crucified for my beliefs and, if I am, you can say, "He
died to make men free."
—MARTIN LUTHER KING JR.

[Self-sacrifice is] an arranged scheme of self-deliverance from evil.
—JOHN OMAN

It is good to be helpful and kindly, but don't give yourself to be
melted into candle grease for the benefit of the tallow trade.
— GEORGE ELIOT

Ye will not attain unto piety until ye spend of that which ye
love. And whatsoever ye spend, God is aware thereof.
— QUR'AN

The enemies of the country and of freedom of the people have
always denounced as bandits those who sacrifice themselves for the noble causes of the people.
— EMILIANO ZAPATA

[Self-sacrifice is] neither amputation nor repentance. It is, in
essence, an act . . . the gift of oneself to the being of which
one forms a part.
— ANTOINE DE SAINT-EXUPÉRY

It is a far, far, better thing that I do, than I have ever done; it
is a far, far better rest that I go to, than I have ever
known.
— CHARLES DICKENS

compassion

The whole idea of compassion is based on a keen awareness of
the interdependence of all these living beings, which are
all part of one another, and all involved in one another.
— THOMAS MERTON

Why stand we here trembling around
Calling on God for help, and not ourselves, in whom God
dwells,
Stretching a hand to save the falling man?
— WILLIAM BLAKE

She did not talk to people as if they were strange hard shells
she had to crack open to get inside. She talked as if she
were already in the shell. In their very shell.
— MARITA BONNER

Spiritual energy brings compassion into the real world. With
compassion, we see benevolently our own human condition and the condition of our fellow beings. We drop
prejudice. We withhold judgment.
— CHRISTINA BALDWIN

Whoever is kind to the creatures of God is kind to himself.
— MUHAMMAD

The love of our neighbor in all its fullness simply means being
able to say to him, "What are you going through?"
— SIMONE WEIL

It is only the happy who are hard, Gilles. I think perhaps it is
better for the world if—if one has a broken heart. One is
quick to recognize it, elsewhere. And one has time to
think about other people, if there is nothing left to hope
for any more.
— HELEN WADDELL

What value has compassion that does not take its object in its
arms?
— ANTOINE DE SAINT-EXUPÉRY

Empathy is not merely the basic principle of artistic creation.
It is also the only path by which one can reach the truth
about life and society.
— NAGAI KAFU

Let no one underestimate the need of pity. We live in a stony
universe whose hard, brilliant forces rage fiercely.
— THEODORE DREISER

Love cannot remain by itself—it has no meaning. Love has to
be put into action and that action is service.
—MOTHER TERESA

One cannot weep for the entire world. It is beyond human
strength. One must choose.
—JEAN ANOUILH

Make some muscle in your head,
but use the muscle in your heart.
—IMAMU AMIRI BARAKA

But a certain Samaritan, as he journeyed, came where he was:
and when he saw him, he had compassion on him,
And went to him, and bound up his wounds, pouring in oil
and wine, and set him on his own beast, and brought him
to an inn, and took care of him.
And on the morrow when he departed, he took out two
pence, and gave them to the host, and said unto him,
Take care of him; and whatsoever thou spendest more,
when I come again, I will repay thee.
—LUKE 10:33–35

There is nothing to make you like other human beings so
much as doing things for them.
—ZORA NEALE HURSTON

Make a rule, and pray to God to help you to keep it, never, if possible, to lie down at night without being able to say: "I have made one human being at least a little wiser, or a little happier, or at least a little better this day."
— CHARLES KINGSLEY

Compassion and nonviolence help us to see the enemy's point of view, to hear his questions, to know his assessment of ourselves. For from his view we may indeed see the basic weaknesses of our own condition, and if we are mature, we may learn and grow and profit from the wisdom of the brothers who are called the opposition.
— MARTIN LUTHER KING JR.

Being unwanted, unloved, uncared for, forgotten by everybody, I think that is a much greater hunger, a much greater poverty than the person who has nothing to eat. . . . We must find each other.
— MOTHER TERESA

If someone listens, or stretches out a hand, or whispers a kind word of encouragement, or attempts to understand a lonely person, extraordinary things begin to happen.
— LORETTA GIRZARTIS

PART IV

PURITY

It will be noted that this entire section about purity ends with but a single quote on the subject. Why should this be?

Think of an absolutely pure pane of glass. What else can you say about it save that you can see through it with perfect clarity?

Yet purity—this clarity—is an extraordinary virtue indeed, and there are ways we can explore the subject through the discussion of its component virtues.

The first on the list of these component virtues is cleanliness. Whether "cleanliness is next to godliness" or not, no one would doubt that there is something *clean* about purity. You cannot see clearly through a dirty glass.

Nor would anyone doubt that cleanliness in turn is related to dignity. We may stretch to see the light of Christ in the disheveled and unwashed, but it does take a stretch, and I imagine the unwashed are unlikely to see that light in themselves. Bathing, when possible, is an act of self-respect as well as one respectful of others.

But what is this about economy and thrift? How are they related? If a man pays his bills on time, has no exorbitant debt, and manages to set a bit aside for a rainy day, we are likely to say that his "affairs are in good order." Conversely, if he fails to practice economy and thrift, his affairs will soon be a mess.

But neatness by itself is hardly synonymous with purity. Is not "the love of money the root of all evil" and thereby inherently impure?

Would that things were so simple! Yes, Jesus did instruct a wealthy young man to sell all he had and give it to the poor.

He did tell us we cannot worship both God and Mammon. But he also said that the poor will always be with us, that we should be wise as serpents and innocent as doves, and he taught through all manner of parables, many of which were about financial investment.

So, without feeling the least bit noble in regard to money (and many other things as well), I early set out upon the path of radical moderation. For this I did have at least some spiritual justification. Jesus was much more wild and weird about it, but the Buddha's central doctrine came to be known as "the Middle Path." By this I understand the Buddha meant not some kind of a watered-down compromise of a life, but rather a life that was able to stretch so as to embrace opposites in a cohesive whole. "You must have the capacity to be sober and the capacity to be intoxicated" was the sort of thing I believe he meant by the Middle Path (not unlike combining wisdom and innocence). As far as money was concerned, I imagine the Buddha might well have said, "Know how to hoard it and know how to give it away." Indeed, he reputedly came to the doctrine of the Middle Path only after an eight-year experiment with asceticism and poverty so radical that it almost killed him. Some have in fact suggested that in statue and painting the Buddha is generally depicted as mildly plump so as to symbolize his ultimate rejection of extreme self-denial.

But why do I call this path of moderation radical? Sensible, perhaps. Obvious, even, but hardly radical. Yet I believe it to be possibly more demanding than the path of radical poverty. I need to resist the temptations of greed on a daily basis. It requires a constant commitment to purity if I am to remain very much "in the world but not of the world." It requires the humility to remember that my money is not really *my* money, but a gift to me from God to be used accordingly. Using it accordingly means with prudence and modesty.

Do not think that this matter of the middle path is simple; it is complex. I have again used the example of money not only because it is so tangible but because it also points out the complexities of purity in a world where people are accustomed to think simplistically of "clean hands untouched by filthy lucre." But I could use innumerable other examples.

For just one instance, take the issue of outspokenness. It has been perhaps fifty years since I last told an outright black lie, a blatant falsehood. Yet still weekly, if not daily, I will withhold a piece of the full truth—what is known as a white lie. By way of example, should someone we find boring invite us to dinner, I may say, "I'm sorry, we can't come. Our son is visiting us that week." It is true that our son is visiting, but that doesn't really mean we can't accept the invitation—or ask if our son can't come along. What I am leaving unspoken is my thought, "We find you boring and would almost rather have influenza than your hospitality."

I am sick of these little white lies. I would dearly love to speak my mind on all occasions; it would be so simple. It would also be destructive, unnecessarily hurting the feelings of many who already have as much pain as they can bear. My most common motive for restraining my exuberant outspokenness is simple courtesy—the primary subject of the section after this one.

Such courtesy is usually not so simple, however. I wish I could say that my motives of courtesy are always pure but, in fact, they are not; they are often highly contaminated. Do I fail to speak my mind solely to avoid hurting my neighbor unnecessarily? Or is it because of my own desire to remain "popular" at all costs? Could it be possible that my neighbor might *need* to have his feelings roughed up a little bit, and that my outspokenness might be an appropriately loving psychological intervention? In this case the failure to speak my mind would be more the result of laziness than love. My real motive would be the desire to avoid the hassle of making waves, waves that often are required to establish a genuine relationship. I could go on and on about the ambiguities of discerning between politeness that is loving and politeness that is a cop-out and basically sinful—just as I could in discerning between the times when soft love is appropriate and when tough love is called for.

How do we make such complex discernments? I don't know for certain. I always distrust myself. But I do have three quite firm guidelines to offer.

One starts with a comment I made in the general introduction to this book to the effect that it may be impossible to distinguish between good loving and good thinking, between thoughtfulness and consideration. Although we may never be able to make the complex discernments of living—ranging from courtesy to money management—with either certainty or perfection, we won't be able to make them at all without thinking about them clearly. Good clear thinking takes time. In several different segments I spend approximately two hours a day in "prayer time." I call it my prayer time to make it sound holy (which it is) so people won't interrupt me. But during it I am seldom praying (as most people envision prayer): I am "merely" thinking, mostly about the everyday decisions I need to make in my life.

Calling this thinking my prayer time is not a falsehood,

and that is my second guideline. You may be smarter than I, but I cannot think clearly without reference to God, a Higher Power, or what some modern philosophers are calling the Ideal Observer (defined as a being who is more knowledgeable than you, more objective, and yet who still cares). So generally what I am doing when I am thinking at these times is checking out the decisions of my life with my Higher Power or Ideal Observer. "Hey, God, how does this look to you through your eyes?" is my constant question or litany.

Finally, I do not know how to do this thinking well without looking at all my impure motives—what Carl Jung called our Shadow. By Shadow he meant the conglomerate of impure motives which we all have but would rather not examine—which we would rather keep in the shadows of our consciousness. Jung and his followers have made it clear that we can never get rid of our "shadow-sides"—our inclination to sin, whether original or not. We are stuck with the dubiousness of our motives. They have also made it clear, however, that the distinction between those human beings who are relatively good and those who are relatively evil is determined by their relative willingness or unwillingness to examine their own Shadows. In other words, the most pure people are most aware of their impurity.

If we are willing to choose this middle path of "being in the world but not of the world," then we must be constantly in touch with our inner demons. The stakes are immense. If we can be up front with our impurities—as outspoken about them as our virtues—then little more needs to be hidden. We will likely develop complicated personalities, but they will become personalities that are relatively *transparent*.

So now we are back to the image of that clean pane of glass. I have two favorite quotes about simplicity. One by Anatole France, contained herein, is "Simple style is like white light. It is complex, but its complexity is not obvious."

The second is attributed to Justice Oliver Wendell Holmes: "I don't give a fig for the simplicity this side of complexity, but I would die for the simplicity on the other side." He was not speaking of simpleminded answers but the clarity that can come only when one has waded through all the complexity that the purity requires. He was almost echoing Jesus, who said, "Blessed are the pure in heart, for they shall see God," meaning, I suspect, that they may actually, eventually, see the other side of all the world's complexity.

cleanliness

Cleanliness and order are not matters of instinct; they are matters of education, and like most great things—mathematics and classics—you must cultivate a taste for them.
— BENJAMIN DISRAELI

Dirt is not dirt, but only something in the wrong place.
— LORD PALMERSTON

Cleanness of body was ever deemed to proceed from a due reverence to God, to society, and to ourselves.
— FRANCIS BACON

Bathe twice a day to be really clean, once a day to be passably clean, once a week to avoid being a public menace.
— ANTHONY BURGESS

Soap and water and common sense are the best disinfectants.
— WILLIAM OSLER

Dignity

Let none presume
To wear an undeserved dignity.
— WILLIAM SHAKESPEARE

Man is not just a stomach. . . . Above all he hungers for dignity.
— JACOBO ARBENZ

There is a healthful hardiness about real dignity that never
dreads contact and communion with others, however
humble.
— WASHINGTON IRVING

Scrubbing floors and emptying bedpans has as much dignity
as the Presidency.
— RICHARD M. NIXON

Economy

On money: Save it when you need it least. Spend it when you
have it most.
— FRANCO MODIGLIANI

I would rather have my people laugh at my economies than weep for my extravagance.

—KING OSCAR II OF SWEDEN

If you want to know whether you are destined to be a success or failure in life, you can easily find out. One test is simple and infallible. Are you able to save money? If not, drop out. You will lose.

—JAMES J. HILL

Any government, like any family, can for a year spend a little more than it earns. But you and I know that a continuance of that habit means the poorhouse.

—FRANKLIN D. ROOSEVELT

Spare no expense to make everything as economical as possible.

—SAMUEL GOLDWYN

The first rule of money management is knowing what you've got. The second is knowing what you want.

—MICHAEL LEVINE

Beware of little expenses; a small leak will sink a great ship.

—BENJAMIN FRANKLIN

Humility

When e're thou speak'st, look with a lowly eye:
Grace is increased by humility.
— ROBERT HERRICK

A fault which humbles a man is of more use to him than a
good action which puffs him up.
— THOMAS WILSON

The more noble, the more humble.
— JOHN RAY

Humility is just as much the opposite of self-abasement as it
is of self-exaltation.
— DAG HAMMARSKJÖLD

Who builds a church to God and not to fame,
Will never mark the marble with his name.
— ALEXANDER POPE

Always remember there are two types of people in this world.
Those who come into a room and say, "Well, here I am!"
and those who come in and say, "Ah, there you are!"
— FREDERICK L. COLLINS

Whoever has in his heart even so much as a rice grain of pride
cannot enter into paradise.
— MUHAMMAD

Better is it to be of an humble spirit with the lowly, than to
divide the spoil with the proud.
— PROVERBS 16:19

The first test of a truly great man is his humility.
— JOHN RUSKIN

Be aware that a halo has to fall only a few inches to be a noose.
— DAN McKINNON

We come nearest to the great when we are great in humility.
— RABINDRANATH TAGORE

He that shall humble himself shall be exalted.
— MATTHEW 23:12

Man was created on the sixth day so that he could not be boast-
ful, since he came after the flea in the order of creation.
— HAGGADAH

Professions of humility are the very cream, the very essence of
    pride; the really humble man wishes to be, and not to ap-
    pear so. Humility is timorous, and starts at her shadow;
    and so delicate that if she hears her name pronounced it
    endangers her existence.
                              —SAINT FRANCIS DE SALES

If only I had a little humility, I would be perfect.
                              —TED TURNER

The meek shall inherit the earth, but not the mineral rights.
                              —J. PAUL GETTY

No man is an island, entire of itself; every man is a piece of the
    Continent, a part of the main.
                              —JOHN DONNE

Life is a long lesson in humility.
                              —J. M. BARRIE

The fact that people do not understand and respect the very
    best things, such as Mozart's concertos, is what permits
    men like us to become famous.
                              —JOHANNES BRAHMS

After all the great religions have been preached and ex-
pounded, or have been revealed by brilliant scholars, or
have been written in books and embellished in fine
language with fine covers, man—all man—is still confronted with the Great Mystery.
—CHIEF LUTHER STANDING BEAR

The greater you are, the more you must practice humility.
—BEN SIRA

Don't be humble. You're not that great.
—GOLDA MEIR

Whatever you may be sure of, be sure of this: that you are
dreadfully like other people.
—JAMES RUSSELL LOWELL

Wait below for he who is above.
—SWAHILI PROVERB

Humility is like underwear—essential, but indecent if it shows.
—HELEN NIELSON

Let us be a little humble; let us think that the truth may not perhaps be entirely with us.
— JAWAHARLAL NEHRU

Meekness (humility) is nothing more than a true knowledge of oneself as one is. Anyone who truly knows himself will be meek (humble) indeed.
— THE CLOUD OF UNKNOWING

modesty

Pocket all your knowledge with your watch, and never pull it out in company unless desired.
— LORD CHESTERFIELD

When anyone remains modest, not after praise but after blame, then his modesty is real.
— JEAN PAUL RICHTER

There are always people in whose presence it is unsuitable to be over-modest, they are only too pleased to take you at your word.
— LOUIS PASTEUR

True modesty does not consist in an ignorance of our merits, but in a due estimate of them.
—Julius Charles Hare and Augustus William Hare

Modesty in human beings is praised because it is not a matter of nature, but of will.
—Lactantius

At least I have the modesty to admit that lack of modesty is one of my failings.
—Hector Berlioz

An impudent fellow may counterfeit modesty, but I'll be hanged if a modest man can ever counterfeit impudence.
—Oliver Goldsmith

The man who is ostentatious of his modesty is twin to the statue that wears a fig-leaf.
—Mark Twain

Make no display of your talents or attainments; for every one will clearly see, admire, and acknowledge them, so long as you cover them with the beautiful veil of modesty.
—Nathaniel Emmons

Modesty: the gentle art of enhancing your charm by pretend-
ing not to be aware of it.
— OLIVER HERFORD

I have offended God and mankind because my work didn't
reach the quality it should have.
— LEONARDO DA VINCI

prudence

If thou thinkest twice before thou speakest once, thou wilt
speak twice the better for it.
— WILLIAM PENN

Be careful of what you ask for; you just might get it.
— ANONYMOUS

Choose your neighbor before your house and your companion before the road.
— ARAB PROVERB

No one tests the depth of a river with both feet.
— ASHANTI PROVERB

Never leave hold of what you've got until you've got hold of
   something else.
                              —DONALD HERTZBERG

It is part of a wise man to keep himself today for tomorrow,
   and not to venture all his eggs in one basket.
                              —CERVANTES

I would rather worry without need than live without heed.
                              —BEAUMARCHAIS

Balancing your budget is like protecting your virtue. You
   have to learn to say, "No."
                              —MICHAEL LEVINE

If thou canst not see the bottom, wade not.
                              —ENGLISH PROVERB

My advice to you, if you should ever be in a hold-up, is to line
   up with the cowards and save your bravery for an occasion when it may be of some benefit to you.
                              —O. HENRY

Although it rain, cast not away the watering pot.
— MALAY PROVERB

If you can't tie good knots, tie plenty of them.
— YACHTSMAN'S CREDO

He who is not a bird should not build his nest over abysses.
— FRIEDRICH NIETZSCHE

If you live in Rome, don't quarrel with the Pope.
— FRENCH PROVERB

Always put off till tomorrow what you shouldn't do at all.
— ANONYMOUS

Consider the little mouse, how sagacious an animal it is which
never entrusts its life to one hole only.
— PLAUTUS

It is well to moor your bark with two anchors.
— PUBLILIUS SYRUS

simplicity

Less is more.
— ROBERT BROWNING

It is proof of high culture to say the greatest matters in the simplest way.
— RALPH WALDO EMERSON

The greatest truths are the simplest: and so are the greatest men.
— JULIUS CHARLES HARE AND
AUGUSTUS WILLIAM HARE

The ability to simplify means to eliminate the unnecessary so that the necessary may speak.
— HANS HOFMANN

The guiding motto in the life of every natural philosopher should be, Seek simplicity and distrust it.
— ALFRED NORTH WHITEHEAD

The obvious is that which is never seen until someone expresses it simply.
— KAHLIL GIBRAN

Our life is frittered away by detail. . . . Simplify, simplify.
—HENRY DAVID THOREAU

Just learn your lines and don't bump into the furniture.
—SPENCER TRACY

Affected simplicity is an elegant imposture.
—LA ROCHEFOUCAULD

Everything should be made as simple as possible . . . but not simpler.
—ALBERT EINSTEIN

Simplicity of character is no hindrance to subtlety of intellect.
—JOHN MORLEY

A child of five would understand this. Send somebody to fetch a child of five.
—GROUCHO MARX

Teach us Delight in simple things.
—RUDYARD KIPLING

Making the simple complicated is commonplace; making the complicated simple, awesomely simple, that's creativity.
— CHARLES MINGUS

You decide what it is you want to accomplish and then you lay out your plans to get there, and then you just do it. It's pretty straightforward.
— NANCY DITZ

I have a simple philosophy. Fill what's empty. Empty what's full. Scratch where it itches.
— ALICE ROOSEVELT LONGWORTH

Sooner or later we all discover that the important moments in life are not the advertised ones, not the birthdays, the graduations, the weddings, not the great goals achieved. The real milestones are less prepossessing. They come to the door of memory unannounced, stray dogs that amble in, sniff around a bit, and simply never leave. Our lives are measured by these.
— SUSAN B. ANTHONY

The art of art, the glory of expression and the sunshine of the light of letters, is simplicity.
— WALT WHITMAN

Simplicity is making the journey of this life with just baggage
enough.
— ANONYMOUS

Life is not complex. We are complex. Life is simple, and the
simple thing is the right thing.
— OSCAR WILDE

God made man simple, but how he changed and got compli-
cated is hard to say.
— JOHANN WOLFGANG
VON GOETHE

True eloquence consists of saying all that should be said, and
that only.
— LA ROCHEFOUCAULD

Simplicity of character is the natural result of profound
thought.
— WILLIAM HAZLITT

The first rule is to keep an untroubled spirit. The second is to
look things in the face and know them for what they are.
— MARCUS AURELIUS

Simple style is like white light. It is complex, but its complexity is not obvious.
— ANATOLE FRANCE

thrift

Spare when you are young, and spend when you are old.
— H. G. BOHN

Keep something for a rainy day.
— PROVERB

Annual income twenty pounds, annual expenditure nineteen nineteen six, result happiness. Annual income twenty pounds, annual expenditure twenty pounds ought and six, result misery.
— CHARLES DICKENS

A penny saved is a penny earned.
— ENGLISH PROVERB

It is better to have a hen tomorrow than an egg today.
— THOMAS FULLER, M.D.

A man who both spends and saves money is the happiest man, because he has both enjoyments.
—SAMUEL JOHNSON

Though you live near a forest, do not waste firewood.
—CHINESE PROVERB

Saving is greater than earning.
—GERMAN PROVERB

purity

Blessed are the pure in heart: for they shall see God.
—MATTHEW 5:8

PART V

PERSEVERANCE

Here, unlike in the introduction to the preceding section, the reader will have no trouble figuring out on her own the components of perseverance: the great virtue of seeing things through.

The word is derived from the Latin prefix, *per,* meaning "by" or "through," and the root word, *severus,* meaning "severe" or "strict." We persevere in this life through the strict practice of commitment, confidence, constancy, conviction, determination, devotion, diligence, and endurance.

The words *strict* and *severe* connote grimness, and I suppose perseverance is often a grim sort of virtue. Like most of the other virtues, it can be carried too far. Indeed, in psychiatry and neurology, we use the verb *perseverate* to describe a kind of pathology. On a biological basis it refers to a particular brain defect that causes its victims to meaninglessly repeat themselves in speech or minor action. Psychologically, it refers to what Freud labeled the "repetition compulsion"—namely, the profound tendency we humans frequently have to do the same stupid thing over and over again, even though it should be obvious that we are butting our heads against a stone wall.

The predominant theme of the quotes that follow is that if we persevere in ways that are not stupid or brain damaged, then we can achieve virtually any goal and succeed at any aim we desire. Great! But what is a right aim or goal? This question is largely left unanswered. So what I would like to focus upon here is the morality of perseverance.

It is noteworthy that the religious—specifically Calvinist Christians—have a special theological definition of perseverance. They define it as "Continuance in a state of grace leading finally to a state of glory." It is, I believe, an excellent definition, but one likely to seem so much gibberish to the theologically untrained, including most Christians. Consequently, I will attempt to translate it.

I have described the moment in my childhood when I first decided to face the music by telling the truth when I probably could have gotten away with a lie. It was at that moment, some Christians would say, that I was "saved." Certainly, I agree it was a moment of personal salvation.

Now for some fine points. Most Christians believe that we are saved by grace alone. In other words, it was God who reached down to me out of His (or Her) graciousness to give me the courage to speak the truth at that moment. With this I largely agree. In attempting to explain the mystery of why some people respond to grace and others don't, the Calvinists developed the doctrine of predestination, declaring that God determined that Scott Peck would be saved long before that moment while also determining that others would never be saved. With this I disagree. Although I have no doubt God helped me at that moment—that I couldn't have done it alone—I also think that I had some free will in the midst of all my fear and trembling. I believe that we are mysteriously cocreators with God in the development of our souls, that God is always trying to help each of us but doesn't have sole say in the matter.

Be that as it may, by God's grace I determined to persevere in telling the truth. When I say "by God's grace," I mean, like all the other virtues, perseverance and its components are largely gifts. Having been supposedly "saved," my journey of pushing myself over the years to speak the truth ever more routinely is what some Christians would call the ongoing work of "sanctification," or actualizing my salvation. My perseverance in doing so would be what the Calvinists meant by "continuance in a state of grace leading finally to a state of glory."

Okay, but what is this state of glory? I suggest it is the only fully worthy goal of perseverance. Since many of those quoted are athletes, it might seem that a state of glory has to do with hitting more home runs than anyone else, with getting your name in the record books. But I have qualms about such a definition; it strikes me as relatively shallow. Does God care much about statistics?

Real glory, I propose, is solely an attribute of God, and we humans can partake of it only in relationship to God. In a famous sermon, entitled "The Weight of Glory," C. S. Lewis put his finger on the matter. Preaching to a throng of students at Oxford at the beginning of World War II—many of whom he knew would soon die in that war, but whose perseverance he wanted to encourage—he said that glory comes only at the end of a long or short life when God says to the individual, "Congratulations. You have done a good job. In you I am well pleased."

Whether I will become fully "sanctified," I have no idea. But it is my abiding hope that when I die I will somehow hear the words: "Congratulations, Scotty. Through your perseverance on behalf of truth you have become the transparent person I hoped, and in you I am well pleased."

Finally, let me return to the matter of how the virtue of perseverance smacks of strictness and severity. Indeed, the

Calvinists have become almost famous—or infamous—for being strict and severe. They have very much been into the *discipline* of perseverance, believing that discipline in and of itself is a sign of the state of grace. What they have generally neglected to emphasize is the extraordinary *freedom* that is the paradoxical result of self-discipline.

One of the component virtues of perseverance, as I have organized them, is diligence. Who would doubt its propriety in the perseverance toward success? The most frequent reason I have failed—or witnessed others fail—in an endeavor has been a lack of due diligence. We have simply failed to devote to the endeavor the amount of time, energy, thoughtfulness, or simple caring that the endeavor required.

The first of the quotes in the chapter "Diligence" is in Latin. It was spoken by St. Augustine at a time when Latin was the closest thing we had to a universal language (English did not yet exist). Because Latin tends to be the most elegantly condensed of languages, this quote is not easily translatable. But I have placed it first because, when I do translate it, I believe you will find it to be simultaneously the most incontrovertible and the most liberating moral prescription ever made.

Dilige, et quod vis fac, it reads. Although somewhat condensed, the last four of the five words are simple. They simply mean: "and what you want do."

Dilige is not so simple. It is declined in the exhortative tense, meaning "Be diligent!" and what St. Augustine meant by this was what I've already mentioned: Take the time, energy, thoughtfulness, and care that the endeavor deserves. It so happens, however, that *dilige* has two other alternative translations from the complex language of Latin. One is the exhortation, "Love!" The other is the exhortation to "Love God." I believe that St. Augustine meant all three in one. If I am correct about this, then his exhortation offers us the greatest of all paths to moral freedom.

Translating his exhortation in its fullest, I think he was saying, "If you are being loving, if you are loving God, and if you are being diligent about it all, then you can do whatever you want. What you do under those circumstances will inevitably be moral and pleasing in the sight of God."

Submission to those three preconditions may seem a strict or severe commitment, even to some Calvinists. To me they seem a small price for the liberation of knowing that I am on the right track.

commitment

I am seeking, I am striving, I am in it with all my heart.
— VINCENT VAN GOGH

The need for devotion to something outside ourselves is even more profound than the need for companionship. If we are not to go to pieces or wither away, we all must have some purpose in life; for no man can live for himself alone.
— ROSS PARMENTER

There are some people whom you have in life who have the capacity for real, passionate commitment to something, and sometimes you may be passionately committed to the same thing. You have to treasure these relationships, and if at times a relationship runs into rocky shoals, you have to treat yourselves as small Eastern European countries and exchange ambassadors. You have to keep that capacity for commitment alive.
— WARREN BEATTY

The quality of a person's life is in direct proportion to his commitment to excellence, regardless of his chosen field of endeavor.
— VINCE LOMBARDI

He is poor indeed that can promise nothing.
—THOMAS FULLER, M.D.

Commit yourself to a dream. . . . Nobody who tries to do
something great but fails is a total failure. Why? because
he can always rest assured that he succeeded in life's most
important battle—he defeated the fear of trying.
—ROBERT H. SCHULLER

You can be an ordinary athlete by getting away with less than
your best. But if you want to be great, you have to give it
all you've got—your everything.
—SWAMI SIVANANDA

confidence

Confidence scarce ever returns to the mind it has quitted.
—PUBLILIUS SYRUS

My mother convinced me to learn to enjoy having people tell
me I can't do something. Now it's second nature; I love
to prove people wrong.
—ANDRE WARE

What fear has he whose account is clean?
— PERSIAN PROVERB

I've always seen myself as a winner, even as a kid. If I hadn't,
I just might have gone down the drain a couple of times.
I've got something inside of me, peasantlike and stub-
born, and I'm in it 'til the end of the race.
— TRUMAN CAPOTE

Search and you will find that at the base and birth of every
great business organization was an enthusiast, a man
consumed with earnestness of purpose, with confidence
in his powers, with faith in the worthwhileness of his
endeavors.
— B. C. FORBES

Never let the fear of striking out get in your way.
— BABE RUTH

You can have anything in this world you want, if you want it
badly enough and you're willing to pay the price.
— MARY KAY ASH

Skill and confidence are an unconquered army.
— GEORGE HERBERT

I can honestly say that I was never affected by the question of the success of an undertaking. If I felt it was the right thing to do, I was for it regardless of the possible outcome.
— GOLDA MEIR

Confidence . . . thrives only on honesty, on honor, on the sacredness of obligations, on faithful protection and on unselfish performance. Without them it cannot live.
— FRANKLIN D. ROOSEVELT

It's so important to believe in yourself. Believe that you can do it, under any circumstances. Because if you believe you can, then you really will. That belief just keeps you searching for the answers, and then pretty soon you get it.
— WALLY "FAMOUS" AMOS

constancy

We should measure affection, not like youngsters by the ardor of its passion, but by its strength and constancy.
— CICERO

There is nothing in this world constant but inconstancy.
— JONATHAN SWIFT

To be capable of steady friendship or lasting love, are the two greatest proofs, not only of goodness of heart, but of strength of mind.
— WILLIAM HAZLITT

It is as foolish to make experiments upon the constancy of a friend, as upon the chastity of a wife.
— SAMUEL JOHNSON

When I am wearied with wand'ring all day,
To thee, my delight, in the evening I come:
No matter what beauties I saw in my way;
They were but my visits, but thou art my home.
— MATTHEW PRIOR

No one can say of his house, "There is no trouble here."
— ASIAN PROVERB

To have a true friendship, you have to do more than exchange Christmas cards or call each other once a year. There has to be some continued support and attention; otherwise the relationship is a sentimental attachment rather than a true friendship.
— DR. DOLORES KREISMAN

There are two sorts of constancy in love, the one comes from the constant discovery in our beloved of new grounds for love, and the other comes from making it a point of honour to be constant.
— LA ROCHEFOUCAULD

It is not best to swap horses while crossing the river.
— ABRAHAM LINCOLN

There are those who would misteach us that to stick in a rut is consistency—and a virtue, and that to climb out of the rut is inconsistency—and a vice.
— MARK TWAIN

Nothing that is not a real crime makes a man appear so contemptible and little in the eyes of the world as inconsistency.
— JOSEPH ADDISON

Men's minds are given to change in hate and friendship.
— SOPHOCLES

Do I contradict myself?
Very well then I contradict myself,
(I am large, I contain multitudes).
— WALT WHITMAN

conviction

It is easier to fight for one's principles than to live up to them.
— ALFRED ADLER

It does not take great men to do great things; it only takes consecrated men.
— PHILLIPS BROOKS

Neutral men are the devil's allies.
— E. H. CHAPIN

Christians have burnt each other, quite persuaded
That all the Apostles would have done as they did.
— GEORGE GORDON, LORD BYRON

We often excuse our own want of philanthropy by giving the name of fanaticism to the more ardent zeal of others.
— HENRY WADSWORTH LONGFELLOW

fanaticism consists in redoubling your effort when you have forgotten your aim.
— GEORGE SANTAYANA

This man will go far for he believes every word he says.
— MIRABEAU OF ROBESPIERRE

Determination

Every man is the son of his own works.
— CERVANTES

Having chosen our course, without guile and with pure purpose, let us renew our trust in God, and go forward without fear and with manly hearts.
— ABRAHAM LINCOLN

You will fetter my leg, but not Zeus himself can get the better
of my free will.
— EPICTETUS

My mother said to me, "If you become a soldier you'll be a general; if you become a monk you'll end up as the pope." Instead, I became a painter and wound up as Picasso.
— PABLO PICASSO

... resolved to take fate by the throat and shake a living out of her.
> — LOUISA MAY ALCOTT

The wisest men follow their own direction.
> — EURIPIDES

Some minds seem almost to create themselves, springing up under every disadvantage and working their solitary but irresistible way through a thousand obstacles.
> — WASHINGTON IRVING

Let us, then, be up and doing,
With a heart for any fate;
Still achieving, still pursuing,
Learn to labor and to wait.
> — HENRY WADSWORTH LONGFELLOW

No farmer ever plowed a field by turning it over in his mind.
> — GEORGE E. WOODBURY

Never give in! Never give in! Never, never, never. Never—in anything great or small, large or petty—never give in except to convictions of honor and good sense.
> — WINSTON CHURCHILL

You can do what you have to do, and sometimes you can do it even better than you think you can.
— JIMMY CARTER

They say you can't do it, but remember, that doesn't always work.
— CASEY STENGEL

The best way out is always through.
— ROBERT FROST

The adults in my life told me I could do anything if I was determined and resourceful. . . . I was expected to be ambitious because there was an intrinsic pleasure in excelling, not because I had to prove anything to whites.
— ERIC V. COPAGE

There is no such thing as a great talent without great willpower.
— HONORÉ DE BALZAC

When the going gets tough, the tough get going.
— JOSEPH P. KENNEDY

Big shots are only little shots who keep shooting.
— DALE CARNEGIE

Even if the doctor does not give you a year, even if he hesitates
about a month, make one brave push and see what can be
accomplished in a week.
— ROBERT LOUIS STEVENSON

Somebody said to me that it couldn't be done
But he with a chuckle replied
That "maybe it couldn't," but he would be one
Who wouldn't say so till he'd tried.
— EDGAR A. GUEST

No matter what you do, do your best at it. If you're going to
be a bum, be the best bum there is.
— ROBERT MITCHUM

To be happy, drop the words *if only* and substitute instead the
words *next time*.
— SMILEY BLANTON

Get a good idea and stay with it. Dog it, and work at it until
it's done, and done right.
— WALT DISNEY

Devotion

God waits to win back his own flowers as gifts from man's hands.

— RABINDRANATH TAGORE

Men are idolaters, and want something to look at and kiss and hug, or throw themselves down before; they always did, they always will; and if you don't make it of wood, you must make it of words.

— OLIVER WENDELL HOLMES SR.

A man cannot make a pair of shoes rightly unless he do it in a devout manner.

— THOMAS CARLYLE

God prefers bad verses recited with a pure heart, to the finest verses possible chanted by the wicked.

— VOLTAIRE

The worship of God is not a rule of safety—it is an adventure of the spirit, a flight after the unattainable.

— ALFRED NORTH WHITEHEAD

And Ruth said, Entreat me not to leave thee, or to return from following after thee: for whither thou goest, I will go: and where thou lodgest, I will lodge: thy people shall be my people, and thy God my God.
— RUTH 1:16

All real joy and power of progress in humanity depend on finding something to reverence, and all the baseness and misery of humanity begin in a habit of disdain.
— JOHN RUSKIN

We adore, we invoke, we seek to appease, only that which we fear.
— VOLTAIRE

I have in my heart a small, shy plant called reverence; I cultivate that on Sunday mornings.
— OLIVER WENDELL HOLMES SR.

Does not every true man feel that he is himself made higher by doing reverence to what is really above him?
— THOMAS CARLYLE

Diligence

Dilige, et quod vis fac.
Love one another, love God diligently, and whatever you do
will be pleasing in the sight of God.
— SAINT AUGUSTINE

Diligence is the mother of good luck, and God gives all things
to industry. Then plough deep while sluggards sleep, and
you shall have corn to sell and to keep.
— BENJAMIN FRANKLIN

He that would eat the fruit must climb the tree.
— JAMES KELLY

To ensure time to think, reflect, and ponder, schedule meet-
ings with yourself and honor them as you would an
appointment with another.
— MICHAEL LEVINE

Know the true value of time; snatch, seize, and enjoy every
moment of it. No idleness, no laziness, or procrastina-
tion: never put off till tomorrow what you can do today.
— LORD CHESTERFIELD

Generally speaking, the great achieve their greatness by
industry rather than by brilliance.
— BRUCE BARTON

My motto is *Nulla dies sine linea*. If I ever let the muse go to
sleep it is only that she may wake refreshed.
— LUDWIG VAN BEETHOVEN

The foot of the farmer is the best manure for his land.
— GERMAN PROVERB

Genius is one percent inspiration and ninety-nine percent
perspiration.
— THOMAS ALVA EDISON

Endurance

People have to learn sometimes not only how much the heart,
but how much the head, can bear.
— MARIA MITCHELL

What cannot be altered must be borne, not blamed.
— THOMAS FULLER, M.D.

folks differs, dearie. They differs a lot. Some can stand things
    that others can't. There's never no way of knowin' how
    much they can stand.
>   — ANN PETRY

I've always found it fascinating that the suicide rate of hand-
    icapped people is far less than of those not handicapped.
>   — MICHAEL LEVINE

It is not miserable to be blind; it is miserable to be incapable
    of enduring blindness.
>   — JOHN MILTON

No pain, no palm; no thorns, no throne; no gall, no glory; no
    cross, no crown.
>   — WILLIAM PENN

Endure, and preserve yourselves for better things.
>   — VIRGIL

For there was never yet philosopher
That could endure the toothache patiently.
>   — WILLIAM SHAKESPEARE

Let's talk sense to the American people. Let's tell them the truth, that there are no gains without pains.
— ADLAI E. STEVENSON

Marrying in the hopes of avoiding conflict and loneliness is like jumping in a lake to avoid getting wet.
— MICHAEL LEVINE

patience

Patience is the companion of wisdom.
— SAINT AUGUSTINE

Patience, that blending of moral courage with physical timidity.
— THOMAS HARDY

To lose patience is to lose the battle.
— MAHATMA GANDHI

Patience caught the nimble hare.
— GREEK PROVERB

We shall sooner have the fowl by hatching the egg than by
    smashing it.
                   — ABRAHAM LINCOLN

Patience can break through iron doors.
                   — YUGOSLAV PROVERB

Though patience be a tired mare, yet she will plod.
                   — WILLIAM SHAKESPEARE

A man must learn to endure that patiently which he cannot
    avoid conveniently.
                   — MICHEL DE MONTAIGNE

A noble, courageous man is recognizable by the patience he
    shows in adversity.
                   — PACHACUTEC INCA YUPANQUI

When you are an anvil, be patient; when a hammer, strike.
                   — ARAB PROVERB

If God has taken away all means of seeking remedy, there is
    nothing left but patience.
                   — JOHN LOCKE

Have patience with all things, but chiefly have patience with yourself. Do not lose courage in considering your own imperfections, but instantly set about remedying them—every day begin the tasks anew.
— Saint Francis de Sales

A wise man does not try to hurry history. Many wars have been avoided by patience and many have been precipitated by reckless haste.
— Adlai E. Stevenson

Patience is a necessary ingredient of genius.
— Benjamin Disraeli

[Patience is] faith waiting for a nibble.
— H. W. Shaw

I do not object to people looking at their watches when I am speaking. But I strongly object when they start shaking them to make sure they are still going.
— Lord Birkett

In doubtful matters courage may do much; in desperate, patience.
— Thomas Fuller, M.D.

It is very strange . . . that the years teach us patience; that the shorter our time, the greater our capacity for waiting.
— ELIZABETH TAYLOR

I am extraordinarily patient, provided I get my own way in the end.
— MARGARET THATCHER

They also serve who only stand and wait.
— JOHN MILTON

The remedy against bad times is to be patient with them.
— ARAB PROVERB

Patience is the companion of wisdom.
— SAINT AUGUSTINE

The future belongs to him who knows how to wait.
— RUSSIAN PROVERB

Prayer of the modern American: "Dear God, I pray for patience. And I want it right now!"
— OREN ARNOLD

Patience is something you admire in the driver behind you,
but not in the one ahead.
— BILL McGLASHEN

Whoever knocks persistently, ends by entering.
— 'ALI

Be patient with a bad neighbor: He may move or face misfortune.
— EGYPTIAN PROVERB

A woman who has never seen her husband fishing doesn't
know what a patient man she has married.
— ED HOWE

The secret of patience: Do something else in the meantime.
— ANONYMOUS

How poor are they that have not patience.
What wound did ever heal but by degrees?
— WILLIAM SHAKESPEARE

Life on the farm is a school of patience; you can't hurry the
crops or make an ox in two days.
— HENRI FOURNIER ALAIN

The most extraordinary thing about the oyster is this. Irritations get into his shell. He does not like them. But when he cannot get rid of them, he uses the irritation to do the loveliest thing an oyster ever has a chance to do. If there are irritations in our lives today, there is only one prescription: make a pearl. It may have to be a pearl of patience, but, anyhow, make a pearl. And it takes faith and love to do it.

—HARRY EMERSON FOSDICK

Never cut what you can untie.

—JOSEPH JOUBERT

Never think that God's delays are God's denials. Hold on; hold fast; hold out. Patience is genius.

—COMTE DE BUFFON

The greatest prayer is patience.

—GAUTAMA BUDDHA

Some people need to be more patient, and some people need to be less patient.

—MICHAEL LEVINE

Long is not forever.

—GERMAN PROVERB

perseverance

Many strokes overthrow the tallest oaks.
— John Lyly

I have nothing to offer but blood, toil, tears and sweat.
— Winston Churchill

Perseverance is more prevailing than violence; and many things which cannot be overcome when they are together, yield themselves up when taken little by little.
— Plutarch

If at first you don't succeed,
Try, try, try again.
— William E. Hickson

I purpose to fight it out on this line if it takes all Summer.
— Ulysses S. Grant

By perseverance the snail reached the Ark.
— C. H. Spurgeon

Whatever I engage in, I must push inordinately.
— ANDREW CARNEGIE

Even the woodpecker owes his success to the fact that he uses
his head and keeps pecking away until he finishes the job
he starts.
— COLEMAN COX

Pray to God, but keep rowing to the shore.
— RUSSIAN PROVERB

The great thing and the hard thing is to stick to things when
you have outlived the first interest, and not yet got the
second which comes with a sort of mastery.
— JANET ERSKINE STUART

I never did anything worth doing by accident, nor did any of
my inventions come by accident; they came by work.
— THOMAS ALVA EDISON

Where I am, I don't know, I'll never know, in the silence you
don't know, you must go on, I can't go on, I'll go on.
— SAMUEL BECKETT

He that would climb the ladder must begin at the bottom.
— GERMAN PROVERB

An apprentice becomes an expert by and by.
— PERSIAN PROVERB

If you cannot take things by the head, then take them by the tail.
— ARAB PROVERB

There was, I thought, something both wonderful and goofy about all this persistent American determination to reform the world. It reminded of the little signs that used to hang in some of the service stores in Dayton, Ohio, when I was a boy. I forget the exact words, but they promised to do anything "possible" by tomorrow but conceded that the "impossible" might take a few days longer. This was the spirit that had conquered the American continent, survived the great economic depression of the '30s, helped restore Western Europe and Japan after World War II and survived the cold war with the Soviet Union for almost half a century.

— JAMES RESTON

If at first you don't succeed, try, try again. Then quit. No use being a damn fool about it.
— W. C. FIELDS

A bar of iron, continually ground, becomes a needle.
>—CHINESE PROVERB

Perseverance is a great element of success. If you only knock long enough and loud enough at the gate, you are sure to wake up somebody.
>—HENRY WADSWORTH LONGFELLOW

If you wish to learn the highest truth, you must begin with the alphabet.
>—JAPANESE PROVERB

Roy has a great asset—20 percent vision. He wears thick glasses with an extra strong lens. So he never sees an obstacle in his path and goes on to success.
>—JOHN TIGRETT

When the rock is hard, we get harder than the rock.
When the job is tough, we get tougher than the job.
>—GEORGE CULLUM SR.

In our day, when a pitcher got into trouble in a game, instead of taking him out, our manager would leave him in and tell him to pitch his way out of trouble.
>—CY YOUNG

Boys, there ain't no free lunches in this country. And don't go
    spending your whole life commiserating that you got the
    raw deals. You've got to say, "I think that if I keep work-
    ing at this and want it bad enough I can have it." It's
    called perseverance.
                                        — LEE IACOCCA

. . . we shall not flag or fail. We shall go on to the end. We shall
    fight in France, we shall fight on the seas and oceans, we
    shall fight with growing confidence and growing
    strength in the air, we shall defend our island, whatever
    the cost may be. We shall fight on the beaches, we shall
    fight on the landing grounds, we shall fight in the fields
    and in the streets, we shall fight in the hills; we shall
    never surrender.
                                    — WINSTON CHURCHILL

No man drowns if he perseveres in praying to God—and can
    swim.
                                    — RUSSIAN PROVERB

When you come to the end of your rope, tie a knot and hang on.
                                — FRANKLIN D. ROOSEVELT

To keep a lamp burning, we have to keep putting oil in it.
                                    — MOTHER TERESA

Without perseverance talent is a barren bed.
— WELSH PROVERB

There are no shortcuts to any place worth going.
— BEVERLY SILLS

You win some, you lose some, and some get rained out, but you gotta suit up for them all.
— J. ASKENBERG

When I was a cub in Milwaukee I had a city editor who'd stroll over and read across a guy's shoulder when he was writing a lead. Sometimes he would approve, sometimes he'd say gently, "Try again," and walk away. My best advice is, try again. And then again. If you're for this racket, and not many really are, then you've got an eternity of sweat and tears ahead. I don't just mean you. I mean anybody.
— RED SMITH

It is not necessary to hope in order to undertake, nor to succeed in order to persevere.
— CHARLES THE BOLD

Consider the postage stamp, my son. It secures success through
its ability to stick to one thing till it gets there.
— Josh Billings

If we are facing in the right direction, all we have to do is
keep on walking.
— Buddhist proverb

Diligence is the mother of good luck.
— Benjamin Franklin

The rung of a ladder was never meant to rest upon, but only
to hold a man's foot long enough to enable him to put the
other somewhat higher.
— T. H. Huxley

I'm inspired when I walk down the street and still see people
trying. A lot of them look as if they're on their last leg,
but they're still getting up somehow.
— Faith Ringgold

Ev'ry day fishin' day, but no ev'ry day catch fish.
— Bahamian proverb

Turn your stumbling blocks into stepping stones.
— ANONYMOUS

Strong people are made by opposition like kites that go up against the wind.
— FRANK HARRIS

Success seems to be largely a matter of hanging on after others have let go.
— WILLIAM FEATHER

I realized early on that success was tied to not giving up. Most people in this business gave up and went on to other things. If you simply didn't give up, you would outlast the people who came in on the bus with you.
— HARRISON FORD

You may have to fight a battle more than once to win it.
— MARGARET THATCHER

Failure is a detour, not a dead-end street.
— ANONYMOUS

As we say in the sewer, if you're not prepared to go all the way, don't put your boots on in the first place.
— ED NORTON

When I thought I couldn't go on, I forced myself to keep going. My success is based on persistence, not luck.
— ESTEE LAUDER

Opportunity is missed by most people because it is dressed in overalls and looks like work.
— THOMAS ALVA EDISON

PART VI

COURTESY

Courtesy evolved from the word *court*. The courts of the kings and queens were traditionally the most supposedly civilized organizations of their day. The people therein lived with an elegance and delicacy beyond the reach of the common man. They set standards for manners and fine dining. They developed codes of etiquette: rules for courtliness and courtesy.

They also developed political backstabbing into a high art and sometimes resorted to outright murder. The courts were not necessarily very nice places.

Our ambivalence about courts is reflected in the word *courtesan*. Literally, courtesan refers to any member of the court. Over the years, however, it has mostly come to be associated with women of the court, and particularly with those who slept around. Today our common understanding of a courtesan ranges from a mistress to a prostitute.

But remember that courtesans are as likely to be male as female and, in an occupational as opposed to sexual sense, just as likely to be prostitutes. Consider diplomats. They are highly educated, well-spoken representatives of the court or the top echelons of a government. But are they necessarily honest? Or true to their convictions? And can it be possible that they don't have any convictions at all? They are usually representatives first and people second. It is their job to represent, not to be themselves. I suggest their primary quality is not their tact so much as their obedience—their obedience to the court as opposed to their own souls or any other Higher Power. How often do they prostitute themselves in the service of mindless obedience, just as Adolph Eichmann did? Actually, it is understandable. They are far more likely to be forgiven for a lapse of tact than a lapse of obedience. Practice a little disobedience and you won't be around at court for very long.

My ambivalence about "the courtly virtues" is such that I once wrote an entire book on the subject. It is subtitled *Rediscovering Civility*. The reason for that subtitle was to rescue the concept of civility from the state of vapidity into which it had fallen. Indeed, the most common dictionary definition of civility is merely that of "superficial politeness." Yet I have been in homes as well as boardrooms watching people ever so politely killing each other, just as at court. It seemed to me that a deeper, more meaningful definition was required.

The definition I finally came up with was that genuine civility is "consciously motivated organizational behavior that is ethical in submission to a Higher Power." Now that's far too much of a mouthful to digest in this little piece, so let me focus on the first two words.

As I wrestled with this definition, one problem was that I knew it was upon occasion proper—indeed, civil—to hurt people's feelings when working together. I was helped to the solution by Oliver Herford, who once said, "A gentleman is one who never hurts anyone's feelings unintentionally." In other words, a key element of real civility is intentionality, by which I mean conscious deliberateness. A gentlewoman may find it necessary to hurt someone's feelings, but she will be fully aware of the consequences when she does so.

Deliberateness is an interesting word. It connotes not only intention but thoughtfulness. To deliberate a matter is to

think about it. And there is a synonym for the verb to deliberate: to consider. From it we derive the noun consideration.
And here, I believe, we have arrived at the heart of things.

Interestingly, consideration is not even listed among the
seventy-nine virtues in this book. I suspect this is because it is
too basic, too fundamental. It undergirds virtually all the others, and perhaps most particularly these courtly virtues of
diplomacy, discretion, tact, and courtesy. If I have criticized
these virtues it is only because they are often practiced unconsciously. They can only be practiced well when done so
thoughtfully—with consideration. In the general introduction to this book I ended with the hope that it would push its
readers to *think*—as it had so pushed me. I extol thoughtfulness above all else, and the greatest of the reasons I eagerly
agreed to edit the book was that it gave me yet another way to
preach consideration.

I preach from experience. The greatest reason that Lily's
and my marriage has managed to survive forty years now is
that we both entered it—even from the earliest days of our
courtship—as two deeply considerate people. From the very
beginning we knew in our hearts the Golden Rule, the great
rule of consideration: "Do unto others as you would have
them do unto you." And we practiced it. We practiced it up
the yazoo.

Only it didn't work out all that well. It was enough to keep
us together—barely—but despite our best intentions, the first
thirty years were marred by quiet yet deep and repetitive conflict. Often it didn't seem fair. Here I was, day after day, year
after year, doing my damnedest to treat Lily as I wanted to be
treated—and she was treating me likewise—and sometimes it

seemed that all we had to show for it was a deep well of mutual resentment. The fact is we were continually and painfully stumbling over each other's best but ignorant intentions.

After twenty-five years of this (isn't it amazing how rapidly we human beings learn!) it began to dawn on us that our ceaseless considerateness had not really been all that thoughtful. It dawned on us not only that she and I were two very different people, but also that it was going to stay that way. Ever so slowly we began to accept each other as being irretrievably different. And that was when we started to realize that the Golden Rule—"Do unto others as you would have them do unto you"—is just the beginner's course. What the advanced course teaches is: "Do unto others as you would have them do unto you, but only if you were in their unique and very different shoes."

This advanced kind of consideration has much more to do with empathy than sympathy. But do not toss it off as an easy, basically emotional virtue. It requires a great deal of actual experience of others and the capacity to not only absorb that experience but also think about it, consider it. Nor do I mean to imply that it is, once learned, anything other than an ongoing and still sometimes painful process. I can say, however, that Lily and I are courting each other these days with a fun-filled efficiency that was quite unimaginable forty years ago.

Diplomacy

I know no diplomacy save that of truth.
— MAHATMA GANDHI

Let every girl, let every woman, let every mother here [in Israel]—and there in my country [Egypt]—know we shall solve all our problems through negotiations around the table rather than starting war.
— ANWAR SADAT

Diplomacy, n. is the art of letting somebody else have your way.
— DAVID FROST

It takes in reality only one to make a quarrel. It is useless for the sheep to pass resolutions in favour of vegetarianism while the wolf remains of a different opinion.
— DEAN WILLIAM R. INGE

I got a call from [Secretary of State General Alexander] Haig, who offered me the job of explaining the Administration's foreign policy to the Chinese—one by one.
— HENRY KISSINGER

The aim of an argument or discussion should not be victory,
but progress.
— JOSEPH JOUBERT

A diplomat is a man who thinks twice before he says nothing.
— FREDERICK SAWYER

A diplomat is a man who always remembers a woman's birthday but never remembers her age.
— ROBERT FROST

Be ye therefore wise as serpents, and harmless as doves.
— MATTHEW 10:16

Discretion

Have more than thou showest,
Speak less than thou knowest.
— WILLIAM SHAKESPEARE

Discretion is valor. A daring pilot is dangerous to a ship.
— EURIPIDES

Questions are never indiscreet: answers sometimes are.
— OSCAR WILDE

The age of discretion is reached when one has learned to be
indiscreet discreetly.
— ANONYMOUS

Remember, a closed mouth gathers no foot.
— STEVE POST

Discretion is the better part of valor.
— ENGLISH PROVERB

A man should live with his superiors as he does with his fire;
not too near, lest he burn; not too far off, lest he freeze.
— DIOGENES

I have never been hurt by anything I didn't say.
— CALVIN COOLIDGE

He knows not when to be silent who knows not when to
speak.
— PUBLILIUS SYRUS

tact

Tact is the intelligence of the heart.
—ANONYMOUS

The most difficult thing in the world is to know how to do a
thing and to watch someone else doing it wrong, without
commenting.
—T. H. WHITE

You never know till you try to reach them how accessible men
are; but you must approach each man by the right door.
—HENRY WARD BEECHER

Tact is after all a kind of mind-reading.
—SARAH ORNE JEWETT

Tact is the ability to describe others as they see themselves.
—ABRAHAM LINCOLN

Keep the other person's well-being in mind when you feel an
attack of soul-purging truth coming on.
—BETTY WHITE

Silence is not always tact and it is tact that is golden, not
silence.
— SAMUEL BUTLER

A tactless man is like an axe on an embroidery frame.
— MALAY PROVERB

A spoonful of honey will catch more flies than a gallon of
vinegar.
— BENJAMIN FRANKLIN

Tact is the art of making a point without making an enemy.
— HOWARD W. NEWTON

Mention not a halter in the house of him that was hanged.
— GEORGE HERBERT

When you shoot an arrow of truth, dip its point in honey.
— ARAB PROVERB

Tact comes as much from goodness of heart as from fineness
of taste.
— ENDYMION

courtesy

A man's own good breeding is the best security against other
people's ill manners.
— LORD CHESTERFIELD

Manners are the happy ways of doing things. . . . If they are
superficial, so are the dewdrops, which give such a depth
to the morning meadow.
— RALPH WALDO EMERSON

To speak kindly does not hurt the tongue.
— FRENCH PROVERB

Never underestimate the power of simple courtesy. Your
courtesy may not be returned or remembered, but dis-
courtesy will.
— PRINCESS JACKSON SMITH

The audience was swell. They were so polite, they covered
their mouth when they yawned.
— BOB HOPE

PART VII

FAITH

My primary identity, before that of a religious person, is that of a scientist. We scientists are empiricists, meaning believers in empiricism. Empiricism is the philosophy that the best—not the only, but the best—route to knowledge is through experience. That is why we conduct experiments—controlled experiences to gain knowledge.

In this respect I am very much like Carl Jung. Toward the end of his long life the media decided to do a film interview with him to capture him for posterity. To me it was a rather inane interview until its conclusion, when the reporter asked, "Professor Jung, a lot of your writings have a religious flavor. Do you believe in God?"

"Believe in God?" old Jung repeated, as best as I can recall, puffing on his pipe thoughtfully. "Well, believe is a word we use when we think that something is true, but for which we do not yet have a substantial body of evidence. No. No, I don't believe in God. I *know* there's a God."

I have faith in God because I have seen the evidence. So, you might say, what is this about faith being a gift, perhaps even more of a gift than any of the other virtues? Later in this book, we will read these words from St. Paul: "By grace are ye saved through faith; and that not of yourselves: it is the gift of God." As far as I am concerned, no truer words were ever spoken. I would simply elaborate that in my personal case it has been God who reached down to me through His grace to open my eyes so that I might see the evidence of His footprints at almost every turn.

Make no mistake; it is a gift. The fact is that many—if not most—people never see the evidence. But how can they not see it? Or hear it? How can they not hear the "still, small voice" of God within them, speaking with a wisdom beyond the capacity of their own brains?

I am reminded of a rather critical review of my early work. The review ended by concluding something to the effect: "These books are not particularly consoling to those of us who do not, like Peck, seem to have a direct phone line to God."

I wrote a note back to the reviewer to suggest that her conclusion might be slightly misleading. "If I have a direct phone line to God," I informed her, "frankly, most of the time the machine doesn't work. But yes, upon occasion it does ring." What I didn't add, out of possibly misplaced kindness, was the fact that many people permanently leave their phone off the hook.

But why? Why would they leave it off the hook? It is an excellent question to which the answers are multiple, complex, and still ultimately mysterious. For the sake of brevity let me simply once more quote St. Paul: "It is a terrifying thing to fall into the hands of the living God." There is a certain loss of control involved that many people either will not or cannot bear.

The ability or willingness to bear it is itself a gift. Yes, faith is indeed a gift. This doesn't mean the gift cannot be sought after and nurtured, however; it most definitely can be. The seeking and nurturance of faith is what I would call "healthy piety."

Piety can be simply defined as "the practice of religious faith." The chapter that follows on this subject is remarkably brief. This is because *public* piety is so frequently not a virtue. Indeed, it is often a vice, an unhealthy practice of self-satisfaction and self-aggrandizement that may actually interfere with faith development. It is no accident that Jesus railed against it. Yet healthy piety is a terribly important matter. Let me redress the poverty of quotes herein by focusing the remainder of this introduction on it, bearing in mind that I shall be talking of piety that is *private,* sometimes even deliberately hidden.

One stumbling block to the silent seeking for God that is healthy piety is the sense of many rational people that they must have God all figured out before they can have faith in Him (or Her). This is understandable but excessively self-reliant. Because God is so much bigger than we are, we can never get Him pinned to the wall like a butterfly we can study at our leisure. You will never completely understand God the way God can understand you. Complete understanding of God as a precondition for faith is an impossible illusion. This is why St. Augustine proclaimed: "Do not seek to understand that you might have faith; seek faith that you might understand." It is a glorious message. Not only does it make the sequence correct, but it rightly implies that the acquisition of faith will open our eyes to a whole new level of understanding.

By agreeing completely with St. Augustine that a healthy faith in God precedes a deep understanding of this world, in no way do I mean to discourage healthy doubt or questioning. In the quotes to follow I deliberately included several that extol doubting. By doubt I don't mean atheism—the certainty that God does not exist. I mean agnosticism—the not-knowing, the questioning of God's ways and even the questioning of His very existence. Such questioning is usually a necessary step in the movement from a simplistic, hand-me-down faith to a faith of mature simplicity that lies "on the other side of complexity." Indeed, I believe that this kind of doubt should be, in itself, considered one of the great religious virtues. Use your mind. Think for yourself, for God's sake!

But do it well. If you are going to get good at this business of doubting, then you are ultimately going to need to learn how to doubt your own doubts. Three decades ago I ran into a strange little gnome of an old man, living in the woods, who had been gifted with a genius for composing couplets of wisdom. One of them was: "If you want to know what God is all about / then why not try giving Him the benefit of the doubt?"

As in this matter of faith preceding understanding, there is another way that my notion of piety was turned topsy-turvy. About a decade ago I happened to run across an ancient Christian proverb, so ancient it was in Latin, reading *"Lex orandi, lex credendi."* Literally translated it says, "The rule of prayer precedes the rule of belief." Until that moment I'd imagined that if I had a lot of faith, then I would pray a lot. But now this proverb was telling me the opposite: that if I prayed a lot, then—and perhaps only then—I would grow in faith. The proverb has the sequence right.

The subject of prayer, or remembering God, is as complex as modern medicine. There are dozens of different ways of praying, and it would be unfitting for me to delve deeply into the complexity here. Suffice it to say that one of the many ways the matter can be categorized is to divide it into public prayer and private prayer. Although public prayer is not without its virtue, herein I am referring to private prayer: the kind of prayer you do alone in your study or bedroom, including prayers of doubt. It is this kind of prayer, usually silent and hidden, that I am preaching as the primary path for seeking the gift of faith or "spiritual growth."

Fifteen years ago I was involved with a team of people that included a young woman I'll call Mary. Mary was then a vocally "fundamentalist" Christian. She seemed unable to speak more than two sentences in sequence without at least one of them including the reverentially intoned name of Jesus. This caused considerable friction. Because I was at the time something of a mentor to her, Mary came to me to ask why she was seemingly alienating the other members of the team.

"It's because of your piety," I explained. "You're so public about it, they feel they're being preached to, and they resent it. They want you as a teammate, not a preacher."

"But what can I do about it?" she inquired in complete innocence.

"What you shouldn't do about it is give up a shred of your faith," I responded. "What you should do is to keep it private. You know," I continued, "I've heard tell of certain Christian monks and nuns who upon occasion practice a strange kind of spiritual discipline. They take a vow—just as they would a vow of poverty or chastity or obedience—to not speak the name of Jesus out loud for a year. They remain free to use his name in their hearts and private prayer, but they renounce their need to speak it publicly. As I said, it's a strange kind of discipline, but I wonder if it wouldn't be a useful one for you at this particular point."

I am unaccustomed to my advice being followed to the letter. But to my amazement, over the year that followed Mary never mentioned Jesus at any team meeting. She rapidly became one of the most successful and constructive team members. After the year she confessed to me she'd not only kept her vow on the team but with all the other friends in her life. "It's bizarre," she said. "Jesus has become ever more important to me over the past year, but I no longer have the slightest need to talk about him."

This has been a mere vignette. But let me say this: I have never seen anyone grow so rapidly, not only in that year but in the years to follow. Indeed, it was not long before Mary had become *my* mentor and one of the greatest spiritual leaders it has been my privilege to know.

enthusiasm

It seems to me we can never give up longing and wishing
while we are thoroughly alive. There are certain things
we feel to be beautiful and good, and we must hunger
after them.

— GEORGE ELIOT

A certain excessiveness seems a necessary element in all
greatness.

— HARVEY CUSHING

In things pertaining to enthusiasm, no man is sane who does
not know how to be insane on proper occasions.

— HENRY WARD BEECHER

I prefer the folly of enthusiasm to the indifference of wisdom.

— ANATOLE FRANCE

The world belongs to the enthusiast who keeps cool.

— WILLIAM MCFEE

Exuberance is Beauty.

— WILLIAM BLAKE

You must learn day by day, year by year, to broaden your horizon. The more things you love, the more you are interested in, the more you enjoy, the more you are indignant about, the more you have left when anything happens.
— ETHEL BARRYMORE

You need to get up in the morning and say, "Boy, I'm going to—in my own stupid way—save the world today."
— SALLY BERGER

Zest is the secret of all beauty. There is no beauty that is attractive without zest.
— CHRISTIAN DIOR

Let us live while we live.
— PHILIP DOORIDGE

The trouble with some women is that they get all excited about nothing—and then marry him.
— CHER

The sense of this word among the Greeks affords the noblest definition of it; enthusiasm signifies "God in us."
— MADAME DE STAEL

Indifference may not wreck a man's life at any one turn, but
it will destroy him with a kind of dry-rot in the long run.
— BLISS CARMAN

God writes my music.
— JOHANN SEBASTIAN BACH

Nothing is interesting if you're not interested.
— HELEN MACINNES

Life is a romantic business. It is painting a picture, not doing
a sum—but you have to make the romance, and it will
come to the question how much fire you have in your
belly.
— OLIVER WENDELL HOLMES JR.

Indifference never wrote great works, nor thought out striking inventions, nor reared the solemn architecture that
awes the soul, nor breathed sublime music, nor painted
glorious pictures, nor undertook heroic philanthropies.
All these grandeurs are born of enthusiasm, and are done
heartily.
— ANONYMOUS

Every production of genius must be the production of
enthusiasm.
—Benjamin Disraeli

Alas! How enthusiasm decreases, as our experience increases!
—Louise Colet

A man can be short and dumpy and getting bald but if he has
fire, women will like him.
—Mae West

If you aren't fired with enthusiasm, you will be fired with
enthusiasm.
—Vince Lombardi

I am not eccentric. It's just that I am more alive than most
people. I am an unpopular electric eel set in a pond of
goldfish.
—Dame Edith Sitwell

When a man dies, if he can pass enthusiasm along to his children, he has left them an estate of incalculable value.
—Thomas Alva Edison

Lack of pep is often mistaken for patience.
—KIN HUBBARD

Don't ever let me catch you singing like that again, without
enthusiasm. You're nothing if you aren't excited by what
you're doing.
—FRANK SINATRA TO HIS SON,
FRANK JR.

If a man is called to be a street sweeper, he should sweep
streets even as Michelangelo painted or Beethoven composed music or Shakespeare wrote poetry.
—MARTIN LUTHER KING JR.

Knowledge is power, but enthusiasm pulls the switch.
—IVERN BELL

It is the greatest shot of adrenaline to be doing what you've
wanted to do so badly. You almost feel like you could fly
without the plane.
—CHARLES LINDBERGH

One can never consent to creep when one feels an impulse to
soar.
—HELEN KELLER

Grace

By grace are ye saved through faith; and that not of yourselves: it is the gift of God.
— EPHESIANS 2:8

Grace is but glory begun, and glory is but grace perfected.
— JONATHAN EDWARDS

Grace fills empty spaces, but it can only enter where there is a
void to receive it, and it is grace itself which makes this
void.
— SIMONE WEIL

Amazing grace! How sweet the sound,
That saved a wretch like me;
I once was lost, but now I'm found;
Was blind, but now I see.
— JOHN NEWTON

Grace strikes us when we are in great pain and restlessness. . . .
Sometimes at that moment a wave of light breaks into
our darkness, and it is as though a voice were saying:
"You are accepted."
— PAUL JOHANNES TILLICH

Grace is not a strange, magic substance which is subtly filtered into our souls to act as a kind of spiritual penicillin. Grace is unity, oneness within ourselves, oneness with God.
— THOMAS MERTON

What is grace? I know until you ask me; when you ask me, I do not know.
— SAINT AUGUSTINE

All men who live with any degree of serenity live by some assurance of grace.
— REINHOLD NIEBUHR

The religious who, of course, ascribe the origins of grace to God, believing it to be literally God's love, have through the ages had the same difficulty locating God. There are within theology two lengthy and opposing traditions in this regard: one, the doctrine of Emanance, which holds that grace emanates down from an external God to men; the other the doctrine of Immanence, which holds that grace emanates out from the God within the center of man's being.
— M. SCOTT PECK

The grace of God is in my mind shaped like a key, that comes
from time to time and unlocks the heavy doors.
— DONALD SWAN

I would like to achieve a state of inner spiritual grace from
which I could function and give as I was meant to in the
eye of God.
— ANNE MORROW LINDBERGH

Give us grace and strength to forbear and to persevere. Give
us courage and gaiety and the quiet mind, spare to us our
friends, soften to us our enemies.
— ROBERT LOUIS STEVENSON

Grace was in all her steps,
Heaven in her eye.
In Every gesture dignity and love.
— JOHN MILTON

It is not in virtue of its liberty that the human will attains to
grace, it is much rather by grace that it attains to liberty.
— SAINT AUGUSTINE

HOPE

While I breathe, I hope.
> —MEDIEVAL PROVERB

"Hope" is the thing with feathers
That perches in the soul—
And sings the tune without
And never stops—at all.
> —EMILY DICKINSON

We must accept finite disappointment, but we must never lose
infinite hope.
> —MARTIN LUTHER KING JR.

Hope is the pillar that holds up the world.
Hope is the dream of a waking man.
> —PLINY THE ELDER

A good hope is better than a poor possession.
> —SPANISH PROVERB

When hope is taken away from a people moral degeneration
follows swiftly after.
> —PEARL S. BUCK

Hope is a risk that must be run.
> — GEORGES BERNANOS

Hope is a prodigal young heir, and Experience is his banker.
> — CHARLES CALEB COLTON

Hope is the source of all happiness. . . . None is to be considered a man who does not hope in God.
> — PHILO

If it were not for hopes, the heart would break.
> — THOMAS FULLER, M.D.

In the time of trouble avert not thy face from hope, for the soft marrow abideth in the hard bone.
> — HAFIZ

Before you focus on finding the right person, concentrate on being the right person.
> — MICHAEL LEVINE

Never give out while there is hope; but hope not beyond reason, for that shows more desire than judgment.
> — WILLIAM PENN

Hope is necessary in every condition. The miseries of poverty, sickness, of captivity, would, without this comfort, be insupportable.
—SAMUEL JOHNSON

Hope has as many lives as a cat or a king.
—HENRY WADSWORTH LONGFELLOW

Hope for the best, but prepare for the worst.
—ENGLISH PROVERB

Hope is the poor man's bread.
—GEORGE HERBERT

The hope, and not the fact, of advancement is the spur to industry.
—HENRY TAYLOR

Hope is a strange invention—
A Patent of the Heart—
In unremitting action
Yet never wearing out—.
—EMILY DICKINSON

In the land of hope there is never any Winter.
— RUSSIAN PROVERB

Hope is the feeling you have that the feeling you have isn't permanent.
— JEAN KERR

There is hope for all of us. Well, anyway, if you don't die you live through it, day in, day out.
— MARY BECKETT

Hope is a very unruly emotion.
— GLORIA STEINEM

If hoping does you any good, hope on.
— C. M. WIELAND

Something will turn up.
— BENJAMIN DISRAELI

The natural flights of the human mind are not from pleasure to pleasure, but from hope to hope.
— SAMUEL JOHNSON

We all hope for a—must I say the word—recipe, we all
believe, however much we know we shouldn't, that
maybe somebody's got that recipe and can show us how
not to be sick, suffer, and die.
— NAN SHIN

Great hopes make great men.
— THOMAS FULLER, M.D.

To eat bread without hope is still slowly to starve to death.
— PEARL S. BUCK

They say Despair has power to kill
With her bleak frown; but I say No;
If life did hang upon her will,
Then Hope had perish'd long ago;
Yet still the twain keep up their "barful strife."
— HARTLEY COLERIDGE

If a man like Malcolm X could change and repudiate racism,
if I myself and other former Muslims can change, if
young whites can change, then there is hope for America.
— ELDRIDGE CLEAVER

More pleasure in hope than in fulfillment.
— JAPANESE PROVERB

There is no medicine like hope, no incentive so great, and no tonic so powerful as expectation of something better tomorrow.
— ORISON MARDEN

Take from a man his wealth, and you hinder him; take from him his purpose, and you slow him down. But take from man his hope, and you stop him. He can go on without wealth, and even without purpose, for awhile. But he will not go on without hope.
— C. NEIL STRAIT

What oxygen is to the lungs, such is hope to the meaning of life.
— EMIL BRUNNER

Everything that is done in the world is done by hope.
— MARTIN LUTHER

The hopeful man sees success where others see failure, sunshine where others see shadows and storm.
— ORISON MARDEN

Cathedrals are an unassailable witness to human passion. Using what demented calculation could an animal build such places? I think we know. An animal with a gorgeous genius for hope.

— LIONEL TIGER

The human body experiences a powerful gravitational pull in the direction of hope. That is why the patient's hopes are the physician's secret weapon. They are the hidden ingredients in any prescription.

— NORMAN COUSINS

Someone once said to me, "Reverend Schuller, I hope you live to see all your dreams fulfilled." I replied, "I hope not, because if I live and all my dreams are fulfilled, I'm dead." It's unfulfilled dreams that keep you alive.

— ROBERT SCHULLER

In Israel, in order to be a realist, you must believe in miracles.

— DAVID BEN-GURION

If one truly has lost hope, one would not be on hand to say so.

— ERIC BENTLEY

To travel hopefully is better than to arrive.
— SIR JAMES JEANS

Hope warps judgment in council, but quickens energy in action.
— EDWARD BULWER-LYTTON

Hope is the gay, skylarking pajamas we wear over yesterday's bruises.
— DE CASSERES

One does not expect in this world; one hopes and pays carfares.
— JOSEPHINE P. PEABODY

The word which God has written on the brow of every man is Hope.
— VICTOR HUGO

Hope is wanting something so eagerly that—in spite of all the evidence that you're not going to get it—you go right on wanting it. And the remarkable thing about it is that this very act of hoping produces a kind of strength of its own.
— NORMAN VINCENT PEALE

Blessed is the man that trusteth in the Lord, and whose hope
    the Lord is.
                —JEREMIAH 17:7

Probably nothing in the world arouses more false hopes than
    the first four hours of a diet.
                —DAN BENNETT

Hope is putting faith to work when doubting would be easier.
                —ANONYMOUS

What can be hoped for which is not believed?
                —SAINT AUGUSTINE

It is necessary to hope, though hope should always be deluded;
    for hope itself is happiness, and its frustrations, however
    frequent, are yet less dreadful than its extinction.
                —SAMUEL JOHNSON

It is the around-the-corner brand of hope that prompts
    people to action, while the distant hope acts as an opiate.
                —ERIC HOFFER

ingenuity

Never tell people how to do things. Tell them what to do and
they will surprise you with their ingenuity.
— George S. Patton

Significant inventions are not mere accidents. . . . Happenstance
usually plays a part, to be sure, but there is much more to
invention than the popular notion of a bolt out of the blue.
Knowledge in depth and in breadth are virtual prerequi-
sites. Unless the mind is thoroughly changed beforehand,
the proverbial spark of genius, if it should manifest itself,
probably will find nothing to ignite.
— Paul Flory

The fellow who invented the life-saver really made a mint.
— Gordon Yardy

Good ideas need landing gear as well as wings.
— C. D. Jackson

There is one thing stronger than all the armies in the world,
and that is an idea whose time has come.
— Victor Hugo

inspiration

A god has his abode within our breast; when he rouses us, the
glow of inspiration warms us; this holy rapture springs
from the seeds of the divine mind sown in man.
—Ovid

There is something in our minds like sunshine and the
weather, which is not under our control. When I write,
the best things come to me from I know not where.
—George Christoph Lictenberg

As I grow older, part of my emotional survival plan must be
to actively seek inspiration instead of passively waiting
for it to find me.
—Bebe Moore Campbell

Listen to the voices.
—William Faulkner

A spur in the head is worth two in the heel.
—Proverb

Ninety percent of inspiration is perspiration.
—Proverb

You can't wait for inspiration. You have to go after it with a
club.
—Jack London

All you have to do is close your eyes and wait for the symbols.
—Igor Stravinsky

Inspiration is the act of drawing up a chair to the writing
desk.
—Anonymous

As long as you're going to think anyway, think big.
—Donald Trump

I dare not alter these things; they come to me from above.
—Alfred Austin

I did not write it. God wrote it. I merely did his dictation.
—Harriet Beecher Stowe

No one was ever great without some portion of divine
inspiration.
—Cicero

Do not quench your inspiration and your imagination; do not become the slave of your model.
—VINCENT VAN GOGH

It usually happens that the more faithfully a person follows the inspirations he receives, the more does he experience new inspirations which ask increasingly more of him.
—JOSEPH DE GUIBERT

What do you do when inspiration doesn't come: be careful not to spook, get the wind up, or force things into position. You must wait around until the idea comes.
—JOHN HUSTON

optimism

I want to see how life can triumph.
—ROMARE BEARDEN

Ah, but a man's reach should exceed his grasp—or what's a heaven for?
—ROBERT BROWNING

The essence of optimism is that it takes no account of the present, but it is a source of inspiration, of vitality and hope where others have resigned; it enables a man to hold his head high, to claim the future for himself and not to abandon it to his enemy.

— DIETRICH BONHOEFFER

I am satisfied with, and stand firm as a rock on, the belief that all that happens in God's world is for the best, but what is merely germ, what blossom, and what fruit I do not know.

— J. G. FICHTE

A pessimist is someone who complains about the noise when opportunity knocks.

— MICHAEL LEVINE

What seems to be a great loss or punishment often turns out to be a blessing. I know, through my own experience, that God never closes one door without opening another.

— YOLANDE D. HERRON

An optimist is a man who starts a crossword puzzle with a fountain pen.

— ANONYMOUS

We cheerfully assume that in some mystic way love conquers all, that good outweighs evil in the just balances of the universe and that at the eleventh hour something gloriously triumphant will prevent the worst before it happens.
—BROOKS ATKINSON

The optimist proclaims that we live in the best of all possible worlds; and the pessimist fears this is true.
—JAMES BRANCH CABELL

The outstanding characteristic of America is the refusal of Americans to accept defects in their society as irremediable.
—LEWIS GALANTIERE

It's simpler to be an optimist and it's a sensible defense against the uncertainties and abysses which otherwise confront us prematurely—we can die a dozen deaths and then usually we find that the outcome is not one we predicted, neither so "bad" nor so "good," but one we hadn't taken into consideration.
—EDWARD HOAGLAND

[Optimism is] making the most of all that comes and the least of all that goes.
—ANONYMOUS

I hold not with the pessimist that all things are ill, nor with the optimist that all things are well. All things are not well, but all things shall be well, because this is God's world.
— ROBERT BROWNING

An optimist is a driver who thinks that empty space at the curb won't have a hydrant beside it.
— *CHANGING TIMES*

Pessimism wilts everything around it.
— MICHAEL LEVINE

An optimist may see a light where there is none, but why must the pessimist always run to blow it out?
— MICHEL DE SAINT-PIERRE

It is worth a thousand pounds a year to have the habit of looking on the bright side of things.
— SAMUEL JOHNSON

If I didn't have spiritual faith, I would be a pessimist. But I'm an optimist. I've read the last page in the Bible. It's all going to turn out all right.
— BILLY GRAHAM

'Twixt optimist and pessimist
    The difference is droll:
The optimist sees the doughnut,
    The pessimist, the hole.
           — MCLANDBURGH WILSON

Let other pens dwell on guilt and misery.
           — JANE AUSTEN

For myself I am an optimist—it does not seem to be much use
    being anything else.
           — WINSTON CHURCHILL

It's such an act of optimism to get through a day and enjoy it
    and laugh and do all that without thinking about death.
    What spirit human beings have!
           — GILDA RADNER

Gray skies are just clouds passing over.
           — DUKE ELLINGTON

We are all in the gutter, but some of us are looking at the stars.
           — OSCAR WILDE

It will all come right in the wash.
— PROVERB

Two men look out through the same bars:
One sees the mud, and one the stars.
— FREDERICK LANGBRIDGE

If you think you'll lose, you're lost,
For out in the world we find
Success begins with a fellow's will;
It's all in the state of mind.

Life's battles don't always go
To the stronger or faster man;
But soon or late the man who wins
Is the man who thinks he can.
— WALTER D. WINTLE

Become a possibilitarian. No matter how dark things seem to
be or actually are, raise your sights and see the possibilities—always see them, for they're always there.
— NORMAN VINCENT PEALE

Optimism doesn't wait on facts. It deals with prospects.
Pessimism is a waste of time.
— NORMAN COUSINS

The greatest discovery of my generation is that a human being can alter his life by altering his attitudes of mind.
—WILLIAM JAMES

When pessimists think they're taking a chance, optimists feel they're grasping a great opportunity.
—ANONYMOUS

Sin is behovely, but all shall be well and all shall be well and all manner of thing shall be well.
—JULIAN OF NORWICH

piety

The strength of a man consists in finding out the way in which God is going, and going in that way too.
—HENRY WARD BEECHER

The great religious texts throughout the ages wouldn't always be exhorting us to do good if they didn't recognize that we're inclined, so often, to do evil.
—MICHAEL LEVINE

Set your affections on things above, not on things on the earth.
— COLOSSIANS 3:2

It is rash to intrude upon the piety of others: both the depth and the grace of it elude the stranger.
— GEORGE SANTAYANA

faith

This I do believe above all, especially in my times of greater discouragement, that I must believe—that I must believe in my fellow men—that I must believe in myself—and I must believe in God—if life is to have any meaning.
— MARGARET CHASE SMITH

faith is, before all and above all, wishing God may exist.
— MIGUEL DE UNAMUNO

As he that fears God fears nothing else, so, he that sees God sees everything else.
— JOHN DONNE

I share Einstein's affirmation that anyone who is not lost on the rapturous awe at the power and glory of the mind behind the universe "is as good as a burnt out candle."
— MADELEINE L'ENGLE

faith is not a formula which is agreed to if the weight of evidence favors it.
— WALTER LIPPMANN

Vigorous questioning can propel a restoration and deepening of conviction. Skepticism is a phase, not an internal condition; out of the embryo of uncertainty grows the examination that produces a deeper, common, more genuine conviction. Paradoxically, it is the very questioning that causes the rubbing that polishes the pearl.
— MICHAEL LEVINE

It is your own assent to yourself, and the constant voice of your own reason, and not of others, that should make you believe.
— BLAISE PASCAL

for as the body without the spirit is dead, so faith without works is dead also.
— JAMES 2:26

faith is the choice of the nobler alternative.
—DEAN WILLIAM R. INGE

faith is a knowledge of the benevolence of God toward us, and a certain persuasion of His veracity.
—JOHN CALVIN

To believe only possibilities is not faith, but mere philosophy.
—SIR THOMAS BROWNE

faith is kept alive in us, and gathers strength, more from practice than from speculations.
—JOSEPH ADDISON

And I said to the man who stood at the gate of the year, "Give me a light that I may tread safely into the unknown." And he replied, "Go out into the darkness and put your hand into the hand of God. That shall be to you better than light and safer than a known way."
—LOUISE HASKINS

faith, like a jackal, feeds among the tombs, and even from these dead doubts she gathers her most vital hope.
—HERMAN MELVILLE

We are not human beings trying to be spiritual. We are spiritual beings trying to be human.
— JACQUELYN SMALL

Yes, I have doubted. I have wandered off the path. I have been lost. But I always returned. It is beyond the logic I seek. It is intuitive—an intrinsic, built-in sense of direction. I seem to find my way home. My faith has wavered but has saved me.
— HELEN HAYES

The most satisfying and ecstatic faith is almost purely agnostic. It trusts absolutely without professing to know at all.
— H. L. MENCKEN

Faith is much better than belief. Belief is when someone *else* does the thinking.
— R. BUCKMINSTER FULLER

You can't solve many of today's problems by straight linear thinking. It takes leaps of faith to sense the connections that are not necessarily obvious.
— MATINA HORNER

I would not attack the faith of a heathen without being sure I
had a better one to put in its place.
—HARRIET BEECHER STOWE

If there was no faith there would be no living in this world.
We couldn't even eat hash with any safety.
—JOSH BILLINGS

There lives more faith in honest doubt,
Believe me, than in half the creeds.
—ALFRED, LORD TENNYSON

Console thyself, thou wouldst not seek Me, if thou hadst not
found Me.
—BLAISE PASCAL

faith embraces itself and the doubt about itself.
—PAUL TILLICH

faith is to believe what you do not yet see; the reward for this
faith is to see what you believe.
—SAINT AUGUSTINE

The world has a thousand creeds, and never a one have I;
Nor a church of my own, though a thousand spires are point-
   ing way on high.
But I float on the bosom of faith, that bears me along like a
   river;
And the lamp of my soul is alight with love for life, and the
   world, and the Giver.
                    —ELLA WHEELER WILCOX

A man consists of the faith that is in him. Whatever his faith
   is, he is.
                    —BHAGAVAD GITA

faith is not a series of gilt-edged propositions that you sit
   down to figure out, and if you follow all the logic and
   accept all the conclusions, then you have it. It is crum-
   pling and throwing away everything, proposition by
   proposition, until nothing is left, and then writing a new
   proposition, your very own, to throw in the teeth of
   despair.
                    —MARY JEAN IRION

Think of only three things—your God, your family, and the
   Green Bay Packers—in that order.
                    —VINCE LOMBARDI

Today you can post the Ten Commandments in Moscow public schools, but it is illegal to do it in the United States.
— MICHAEL LEVINE

I respect faith, but doubt is what gets you an education.
— WILSON MIZNER

The great act of faith is when man decides that he is not God.
— OLIVER WENDELL HOLMES JR.

We live by faith or we do not live at all. Either we venture—or we vegetate. If we venture, we do so by faith simply because we cannot know the end of anything at its beginning. We risk marriage on faith or we stay single. We prepare for a profession by faith or we give up before we start. By faith we move mountains of opposition or we are stopped by molehills.
— HAROLD WALKER

A person can do other things against his will; but belief is possible only in one who is willing.
— SAINT AUGUSTINE

My reason nourishes my faith and my faith my reason.
— NORMAN COUSINS

If you have any faith, give me, for heaven's sake, a share of it!
Your doubts you may keep to yourself, I have plenty of
my own.
— JOHANN WOLFGANG VON GOETHE

faith is the antiseptic of the soul.
— WALT WHITMAN

Let us have faith that right makes might; and in that faith let
us dare to do our duty as we understand it.
— ABRAHAM LINCOLN

I do not feel obliged to believe that the same God who has en-
dowed us with sense, reason, and intellect, has intended
us to forgo their use.
— GALILEO

It is consciousness itself . . . which can suggest that there is
God. For it is the hint that there can exist something very
real that is more than the merely physical.
— BARRY HOLTZ

Treat the other man's faith gently; it is all he has to believe
with.
— HENRY S. HASKINS

Conversion for me was not a Damascus Road experience. I
slowly moved into an intellectual acceptance of what my
intuition had always known.
— MADELEINE L'ENGLE

faith is never identical with piety.
— KARL BARTH

I would rather live in a world where my life is surrounded by
mystery than live in a world so small that my mind could
comprehend it.
— HARRY EMERSON FOSDICK

Skepticism is the beginning of faith.
— GEORGE BERNARD SHAW

If you can't have faith in what is held up to you for faith, you
must find things to believe in yourself, for a life without
faith in something is too narrow a space to live.
— GEORGE E. WOODBURY

We must have infinite faith in each other. If we have not, we
must never let it leak out that we have not.
— HENRY DAVID THOREAU

faith is not *being sure*. It is *not being sure,* but betting with your last cent.
— MARY JEAN IRION

We have not lost faith, but we have transferred it from God to the medical profession.
— GEORGE BERNARD SHAW

A faith that cannot survive collision with the truth is not worth many regrets.
— ARTHUR C. CLARKE

The twenty-first century will be religious or will not be at all.
— ANDRÉ MALRAUX

Question with boldness even the existence of God; because, if there be one, he must more approve of the homage of reason than that of blindfolded fear.
— THOMAS JEFFERSON

There is one thing higher than Royalty: and that is religion, which causes us to leave the world, and seek God.
— ELIZABETH I

People see God every day. They just don't recognize him.
— PEARL BAILEY

'Twant me, 'twas the Lord. I always told Him, "I trust you. I
don't know where to go or what to do, but I expect you
to lead me." And He always did.
— HARRIET TUBMAN

Faith affirms what the senses do not affirm, but not the contrary
of what they perceive. It is above, and not contrary to.
— BLAISE PASCAL

Every human being is born without faith. Faith comes only
through the process of making decisions to change before
we can be sure it's the right move.
— DR. ROBERT SCHULLER

Faith is not making religious-sounding noises in the daytime.
It is asking your inmost self questions at night—and then
getting up and going to work.
— MARY JEAN IRION

Faith is the belief of the heart in that knowledge which comes
from the Unseen.
— MUHAMMAD BEN KAFIF

PART VIII

GOODNESS

Much of this section on human goodness is about honesty and truthfulness because I believe they are of such importance. They can also be tricky, which is why I've deliberately included two ringing quotes of President ("tricky Dick") Nixon extolling truthfulness.

Bear in mind we would not—sincerely or insincerely—extol truthfulness and honesty as virtues were there not dishonest people aplenty in the world. Indeed, we would not even possess the notion of goodness without its counterpoint of badness or evil.

I believe that Genesis 3 is, among other things, a marvelous myth about our evolution into consciousness and free will. The first thing that happened after Adam and Eve ate of the fruit of the Tree of Knowledge of Good and Evil is that they became conscious—specifically self-conscious and hence aware of their nakedness. I also believe this was the moment they became human. Without the knowledge of good and evil how can there be free will? It is said that God created us in His own image, and I think above everything else this means that He gave us free will, the freedom to choose either for good or for ill. Evil is an inevitable consequence of this freedom.

It is not accident, I suspect, that the very next story, Genesis 4, is one of murder. And of lying. When God asked Cain where his brother Abel was, Cain didn't truthfully answer, "I killed him, and buried him in the underbrush over there." Instead he responded with a deceitful and irrelevant question: "Am I my brother's keeper?" Tricky! Conscious of the fact he had committed evil, Cain immediately resorted to an attempted cover-up.

The quotes that follow about goodness speak for themselves. Consequently, I am going to speak primarily about evil, the other side of the coin. It is not a popular subject these days. Most people would rather not look at it; many even deny that evil exists. But the very first quote reads: "The thin precarious crust of decency is all that separates any civilization, however impressive, from the hells of anarchy or systematic tyranny which lie in wait beneath the surface." I suggest that the denial of the reality of evil—and our underlying proclivity to it—is extremely hazardous. We must never take decency totally for granted. Otherwise, we are likely to end up condoning indecency.

We do not necessarily know the reasons for our underlying proclivity to evil. This is why St. Paul referred to "the mystery of iniquity." Is it just that we are tainted by original sin? Does the devil have any role to play in it? I honestly don't know.

On the basis of experience with two exorcisms I happen to believe the devil exists. I put forth my belief in a small chapter on demonic possession in my much larger book about evil, *People of the Lie.* An old classmate read it and wrote me the following letter.

Not long after we were in college together I became an alcoholic. Four years ago I joined Alcoholics Anonymous, and I have been sober ever since. The last year, however, has been quite stressful, and for the past two months I had been literally planning to go on a binge again. But then I read your book. As an AA member I believe in the existence of a Higher Power. After finishing your chapter on possession and exorcism, for the first time in my life I wondered whether there might be such a thing as a "lower power." I found the concept to not only be intriguing but for me personally helpful. I am no longer planning that binge, and I wanted to write to thank you for your contribution to me.

I have no desire to convert anyone to a belief in the devil, but I do desire to convert all to a belief in a "lower power." Or call it your Shadow or "shadow-side," if you will, but do get in touch with it; do become aware of its existence. Such awareness will be helpful to you and to others around you, as a number of the following quotes suggest. Awareness of your own potential for evil is the best preventative for committing it.

The two possessed patients I saw were in deep spiritual conflict, but they were not evil. What role the devil might play in human affairs other than its involvement in a very few, extremely rare cases of genuine possession, I don't have the foggiest idea. But that there are truly evil people in some abundance I know for a fact. Make no mistake about it: There are people out there who like to hurt others, physically or mentally, who *like* to torture or otherwise crush others, who want to destroy anything that is good, who delight in lying and see it as a sport, and who are actually prideful of their capacity for deception. Deny this reality at your peril.

In some ways I do not find this reality particularly mysterious. The prevailing Judeo-Christian vision is that this is a naturally good world that somehow mysteriously became contaminated by evil. Despite identifying myself as a Christian, my own vision is the opposite: This is a naturally evil world that has somehow—mysteriously and miraculously—become contaminated by goodness.

Regard young children. We rejoice in their smooth, soft skin, their zest and spontaneity. But they are also all born liars, thieves, cheats, and manipulators. It is hardly remarkable that many of them grow up to become adult liars, cheats, thieves, and manipulators. What is more difficult to explain is why or how the majority of them grow up for the most part to become decent, honest, God-fearing, good citizens.

So, while I too am impressed by "the mystery of iniquity," I am far more thunderstruck by the awesome mystery of human goodness.

As a result, I am mostly an optimist. This is not to say that there aren't days when I despair for the human race. On most days, however, I not only believe that this world has been "contaminated" by an infection of goodness, but that the good bugs are multiplying, and that in the end this strange infection of goodness will take over. I believe this primarily when I manage to keep my eye on the big picture. The facts are there. For instance, three thousand years ago prisoners of war were ritually and customarily disemboweled. Such behavior still occurs, but it is an aberration rather than a norm, and perpetrators may well be prosecuted for war crimes (the latter being a remarkably recent concept). Ever so slowly, almost imperceptibly, our standards of decency seem to be rising.

But how did the good bugs get here? From whence cometh this strange, gradual infection of goodness? Given my knowledge of supposed human nature, of its inherent narcissism and laziness, I can offer a somewhat fair explanation of human evil without having to resort to the existence of the devil. But I cannot even begin to explain the mystery of human goodness without resorting to God.

Which brings me back to my repeated refrain of virtues as gifts. And back from a focus on evil to the greater subject of goodness. And to a certain moral: Insofar as we are good, I think we'd be wise to thank God for it being so.

Decency

The thin precarious crust of decency is all that separates any civilization, however impressive, from the hells of anarchy or systematic tyranny which lie in wait beneath the surface.
—ALDOUS HUXLEY

Pay quickly with what thou owest. The needy tradesman is made glad by such considerate haste.
—WALTER SMITH

Never give unnecessary pain. The cricket is not the nightingale; why tell him so? Throw yourself into the mind of the cricket . . . it is what charity commands.
—HENRI FRÉDÉRIC AMIEL

Our society allows people to be absolutely neurotic and totally out of touch with their feelings and everyone else's feelings, and yet be very respectable.
—NTOZAKE SHANGE

You can't say yes to everything. When you do say yes, say it quickly. But always take a half hour to say no, so you can understand the other fellow's side too.
—FRANCIS CARDINAL SPELLMAN

Advice and reprehension require the utmost delicacy; and
painful truths should be delivered in the softest terms. . . .
A courteous man will mix what is conciliating with what
is offensive; praise, with censure. . . . Advice, divested of
the harshness and yet retaining the honest warmth of
truth, "is like the honey put around the brim of a vessel
full of wormwood."
— WILLIAM COWPER

Harmony

How much finer things are in composition than alone.
— RALPH WALDO EMERSON

It is indeed from the experience of beauty and happiness, from
the occasional harmony between our nature and our environment, that we draw our conception of the divine life.
— GEORGE SANTAYANA

How can people say one skin is colored when each has its own
coloration? What should it matter that one bowl is dark
and the other pale, if each is of good design and serves its
purpose well? We who are clay blended by the Master
Potter come from the kiln of Creation in many hues.
— POLINGAYSI QOYAWAYMA

That sort of beauty which is called natural, as of vines, plants, trees, etc., consists of a very complicated harmony; and all the natural motions, and tendencies, and figures of bodies in the universe are done according to proportion, and therein is their beauty.
— JONATHAN EDWARDS

Harmony would lose its attractiveness if it did not have a background of discord.
— TEHYI HSIEH

Dust as we are, the immortal spirit grows
Like harmony in music; there is a dark
Inscrutable workmanship that reconciles
Discordant elements, makes them cling together
In one society.
— WILLIAM WORDSWORTH

If we do not work at releasing the inharmonious thoughts and attitudes that grow deep within, there is nothing that mere physical release can do for us.
— JULIETTE MCGINNIS

The movement of life has its rest in its own music.
— RABINDRANATH TAGORE

Honesty

Honesty is the first chapter of the book of wisdom.
— THOMAS JEFFERSON

An honest man's word is as good as his bond.
— CERVANTES

Heav'n that made me honest, made me more
Than ever king did, when he made a lord.
— NICHOLAS ROWE

Who cannot open an honest mind
No friend will he be of mine.
— EURIPIDES

I hope I shall always possess firmness and virtue enough to
maintain what I consider the most enviable of all titles,
the character of an "Honest Man."
— GEORGE WASHINGTON

In an honest man there is always something of a child.
— MARTIAL

If people would dare to speak to one another unreservedly, there would be a good deal less sorrow in the world a hundred years hence.
— SAMUEL BUTLER

To state the facts frankly is not to despair for the future nor indict the past.
— JOHN F. KENNEDY

Of all crafts, to be an honest man is the master craft.
— JOHN RAY

Honest men fear neither the light nor the dark.
— THOMAS FULLER, M.D.

I do not remember that in my whole life I ever willfully misrepresented anything to anybody at any time. I have never knowingly had connection with a fraudulent scheme.
— J. P. MORGAN

I liked the store detective who said he'd seen a lot of people who were so confused that they'd stolen things, but never one so confused that they'd paid twice.
— BARONESS PHILLIPS

It is inaccurate to say I hate everything. I am strongly in favor of common sense, common honesty, and common decency. This makes me forever ineligible for any public office.
— H. L. MENCKEN

There is only one way to find out if a man is honest—ask him. If he says "yes," you know he's crooked.
— GROUCHO MARX

A man can build a staunch reputation for honesty by admitting he was in error, especially when he gets caught at it.
— ROBERT RUARK

God looks at the clean hands, not the full ones.
— PUBLILIUS SYRUS

No legacy is so rich as honesty.
— WILLIAM SHAKESPEARE

Honesty pays, but it don't seem to pay enough to suit some people.
— KIN HUBBARD

An honest God is the noblest work of man.
— ROBERT G. INGERSOLL

Whatever games are played with us, we must play no games
with ourselves, but deal in our privacy with the last honesty and truth.
— RALPH WALDO EMERSON

A commentary on the times is that the word "honesty" is now
preceded by "old-fashioned."
— LARRY WOLTERS

An honest man's the noblest work of God.
— ALEXANDER POPE

Honesty is the best policy.
— ENGLISH PROVERB

If he does really think that there is no distinction between vice
and virtue, when he leaves our houses let us count our
spoons.
— SAMUEL JOHNSON

We must make the world honest before we can honestly say to our children that honesty is the best policy.
— GEORGE BERNARD SHAW

Is there anything worse than an insincere smile?
— MICHAEL LEVINE

He who says there is no such thing as an honest man, you may be sure is himself a knave.
— BISHOP BERKELEY

A shady business never yields a sunny life.
— B. C. FORBES

Never esteem anything as of advantage to thee that shall make thee break thy word or lose thy self-respect.
— MARCUS AURELIUS

The art of life is to show your hand. There is no diplomacy like candor. You may lose by it now and then, but it will be a loss well gained if you do. Nothing is so boring as having to keep up a deception.
— E. V. LUCAS

Honor

If I lose mine honor,
I lose myself.

— WILLIAM SHAKESPEARE

Fame is something that must be won; honor is something that
must not be lost.

— ANONYMOUS

I could not love thee, dear, so much,
Loved I not honor more.

— RICHARD LOVELACE

That I may have a constant regard to honor and probity, that
I may possess a perfect innocence and a good conscience,
and at length become truly virtuous and magnani-
mous,—help me, good God; help me, O Father!

— BENJAMIN FRANKLIN

It is better to deserve honors and not have them than to have
them and not deserve them.

— MARK TWAIN

integrity

Let us be true: this is the highest maxim of art and of life, the secret of eloquence and of virtue, and of all moral authority.

— HENRI FRÉDÉRIC AMIEL

You cannot drive straight on a twisting lane.

— RUSSIAN PROVERB

A little integrity is better than any career.

— RALPH WALDO EMERSON

Nothing so completely baffles one who is full of trick and duplicity himself, than straightforward and simple integrity in another.

— CHARLES CALEB COLTON

Would that the simple maxim, that honesty is the best policy, might be laid to heart; that a sense of the true aim of life might elevate the tone of politics and trade till public and private honor became identical.

— MARGARET FULLER

Integrity without knowledge is weak and useless, and knowledge without integrity is dangerous and dreadful.
— SAMUEL JOHNSON

A gentleman is one who keeps his promises to those who cannot enforce them.
— ANONYMOUS

To be individually righteous is the first of all duties, come
what may to one's self, to one's country, to society, and to
civilization itself.
— JOSEPH WOOD KRUTCH

Wisdom and virtue are like the two wheels of a cart.
— JAPANESE PROVERB

It is better to be true to what you believe, though that be
wrong, then to be false to what you believe, even if that
belief is correct.
— ANNA HOWARD SHAW

He has honor if he holds himself to an ideal of conduct
though it is inconvenient, unprofitable, or dangerous to
do so.
— WALTER LIPPMANN

You cannot throw words like heroism and sacrifice and nobility and honor away without abandoning the qualities they express.

— MARYA MANNES

So long as you write what you wish to write, that is all that matters; and whether it matters for ages or only for hours, nobody can say. But to sacrifice a hair of the head of your vision, a shade of its colour, in deference to some Headmaster with a silver pot in his hand, or to some professor with a measuring-rod up his sleeve, is the most abject treachery, and the sacrifice of wealth and chastity, which used to be said to be the greatest of human disasters, a mere flea-bite in comparison.

— VIRGINIA WOOLF

I cannot and will not cut my conscience to fit this year's fashions.

— LILLIAN HELLMAN

This above all: to thine own self be true,
And it must follow, as the night the day,
Thou canst not then be false to any man.

— WILLIAM SHAKESPEARE

How happy is he born and taught,
That serveth not another's will;
Whose armour is his honest thought,
And simple truth his utmost skill.
— SIR HENRY WOTTON

Without being bound to the fulfillment of promises, we
    would never be able to keep our identities; we would be
    condemned to wander helplessly and without direction
    in the darkness of each man's lonely heart, caught in its
    contradictions and equivocalities—a darkness which
    only the light shed over the public realm through the
    presence of others, who confirm the identity between the
    one who promises and the one who fulfills, can dispel.
— HANNAH ARENDT

Loyalty

We are all in the same boat in a stormy sea, and we owe each
    other a terrible loyalty.
— G. K. CHESTERTON

Whose bread I eat, his song I sing.
— GERMAN SAYING

An ounce of loyalty is worth a pound of cleverness.
— ELBERT HUBBARD

Had I but served God as diligently as I have served the king,
he would not have given me over in my gray hairs.
— CARDINAL WOLSEY

Loyalty is the one thing a leader cannot do without.
— A. P. GOUTHEY

To be sure, the dog is loyal. But why, on that account, should
we take him as an example? He is loyal to men, not to
other dogs.
— KARL KRAUS

A man who will steal *for* me will steal *from* me.
— THEODORE ROOSEVELT

If this man is not faithful to his God, how can he be faithful
to me, a mere man?
— THEODORIC

sincerity

A friend is a person with whom I may be sincere. Before him
I may think aloud.
— RALPH WALDO EMERSON

Be as you would seem to be.
— THOMAS FULLER, M.D.

What comes from the heart, goes to the heart.
— SAMUEL TAYLOR COLERIDGE

The primary condition for being sincere is the same as for
being humble: not to boast of it, and probably not even to
be aware of it.
— HENRI PEYRE

To be sincere is to be nude.
— ANONYMOUS

A man must not always tell all, for that were folly: but what a
man says should be what he thinks.
— MICHEL DE MONTAIGNE

Suit the action to the word, the word to the action.
—WILLIAM SHAKESPEARE

The most exhausting thing in life, I have discovered, is being
    insincere.
—ANNE MORROW LINDBERGH

Men are always sincere. They change sincerities, that's all.
—TRISTAN BERNARD

Nothing astonishes men so much as common sense and plain
    dealing.
—RALPH WALDO EMERSON

Truthfulness

Veracity is the heart of morality.
—THOMAS HENRY HUXLEY

To be wiser than other men is to be honester than they; and
    strength of mind is only courage to see and speak the
    truth.
—WILLIAM HAZLITT

Truth is a jewel which should not be painted over; but it may
be set to advantage and shown in a good light.
— GEORGE SANTAYANA

Peace if possible, but truth at any rate.
— MARTIN LUTHER

As scarce as truth is, the supply has always been in excess of
the demand.
— HENRY WHEELER SHAW

I speak truth, not so much as I would, but as much as I dare;
and I dare a little the more, as I grow older.
— MICHEL DE MONTAIGNE

If you tell the truth you don't have to remember anything.
— MARK TWAIN

Truth is the daughter of God.
— ENGLISH PROVERB

The highest compact we can make with our fellow man is,
"Let there be truth between us two for evermore."
— RALPH WALDO EMERSON

The most casual student of history knows that, as a matter of fact, truth does not necessarily vanquish. What is more, truth can never win unless it is promulgated. Truth does not carry within itself an antitoxin to falsehood. The cause of truth must be championed, and it must be championed dynamically.

— WILLIAM F. BUCKLEY JR.

Comment is free but facts are sacred.

— CHARLES SCOTT

It takes two to speak the truth—one to speak, and another to hear.

— HENRY DAVID THOREAU

There is no worse lie than a truth misunderstood by those who hear it.

— WILLIAM JAMES

The truth is America's most potent weapon. We cannot enlarge upon the truth. But we can and must intensify our efforts to make that truth more shining.

— RICHARD M. NIXON

When in doubt, tell the truth.

— MARK TWAIN

One should accept the truth from whatever source it proceeds.
— MAIMONIDES

Truth keeps the hand cleaner than soap.
— WEST AFRICAN PROVERB

One truth discovered, one pang of regret at not being able to
express it, is better than all the fluency and flippancy in
the world.
— WILLIAM HAZLITT

The best way to show that a stick is crooked is not to argue
about it or to spend time denouncing it, but to lay a
straight stick alongside it.
— D. L. MOODY

We shall return to proven ways—not because they are old,
but because they are true.
— BARRY GOLDWATER

Truth is always strong, no matter how weak it looks, and
falsehood is always weak, no matter how strong it looks.
— PHILLIPS BROOKS

A tongue's slip is a truth's revelation.
— GREEK PROVERB

Chase after the truth like all hell and you'll free yourself, even though you never touch its coat-tails.
— CLARENCE DARROW

Some people handle the truth carelessly;
Others never touch it at all.
— ANONYMOUS

Truth is something you stumble into when you think you're going someplace else.
— JERRY GARCIA

And ye shall know the truth, and the truth shall make you free.
— JOHN 8:32

A society committed to the search for truth must give protection to, and set a high value upon, the independent and original mind, however angular, however rasping, however socially unpleasant it may be; for it is upon such minds, in large measure, that the effective search for truth demands.
— CARYL P. HASKINS

Accustom your children to a strict attention to Truth, even in the most minute particulars. If a thing happened at one window, and they, when relating it, say that it happened at another, do not let it pass, but instantly check them: you do not know where deviations from Truth will end.
— SAMUEL JOHNSON

As best you can, stare the truth in the face.
— RICHARD VON WEIZSACKER

Believe those who are seeking the truth; doubt those who find it.
— ANDRÉ GIDE

It makes all the difference in the world whether we put truth in the first place, or in the second place.
— JOHN MORLEY

For my part, whatever anguish of spirit it may cost, I am willing to know the whole truth—to know the worst and provide for it.
— PATRICK HENRY

I tore myself away from the safe comfort of certainties through my love for truth; and truth rewarded me.
— SYLVIA ASHTON-WARNER

Let us begin by committing ourselves to the truth—to see it as it is, and tell it like it is—to find the truth, to speak the truth, and to live the truth.
— RICHARD M. NIXON

I never give 'em hell. I just tell the truth and they think it's hell.
— HARRY S. TRUMAN

Every truth passes through three stages before it is recognized. In the first it is ridiculed, in the second it is opposed, in the third it is regarded as self-evident.
— ARTHUR SCHOPENHAUER

No one can bar the road to truth, and to advance its cause I'm ready to accept even death.
— ALEKSANDR SOLZHENITSYN

The truth is rarely pure and never simple. Modern life would be very tedious if it were either, and modern literature a complete impossibility.
— OSCAR WILDE

If God were able to backslide from truth I would fain cling to truth and let God go.
— MEISTER ECKHART

I cannot prove scientifically that truth must be conceived as a
truth that is valid independent of humanity; but I believe
it firmly.
— ALBERT EINSTEIN

There is no God higher than Truth.
— MAHATMA GANDHI

Truth is the beginning of every good thing, both in Heaven
and on earth; and he who would be blessed and happy
should be from the first a partaker of the truth, for then
he can be trusted.
— PLATO

The opposite of a correct statement is a false statement. But
the opposite of a profound truth may well be another
profound truth.
— NIELS BOHR

Fraud and falsehood only dread examination. Truth invites it.
— THOMAS COOPER

Poetry is not the assertion of truth, but the making of that
truth more fully real to us.
— T. S. ELIOT

There's an element of truth in every idea that lasts long
enough to be called corny.
— IRVING BERLIN

I have come to the conclusion that a person should never
accept any statement or even fact as being the absolute
truth. . . . No statement should be believed merely
because it has been made by an authority.
— HANS REICHENBACH

virtue

There is plenty of evidence for an Original Virtue underlying
Original Sin. . . . The knowledge that there is a central
chamber of the soul, blazing with the light of divine love
and wisdom, has come, in the course of history, to multitudes of human beings.
— ALDOUS HUXLEY

Beauty without virtue is a flower without perfume.
— FRENCH PROVERB

The moral virtues are habits, and habits are formed by acts.
— ROBERT M. HUTCHINS

Virtue is not to be considered in the light of mere innocence, or abstaining from harm; but as the exertion of our faculties in doing good.
— JOSEPH BUTLER

It has been my experience that people who have no vices have very few virtues.
— ABRAHAM LINCOLN

To bring forth and preserve, to produce without possessing, to act without hope of reward, and to expand without waste, this is the supreme virtue.
— LAO-TZU

Virtue is the art of the whole life.
— PHILO

Virtue is its own reward, but it's very satisfactory when Providence throws in some little additional bonus.
— *WOMAN'S HOME COMPANION*

I know only that what is moral is what you feel good after and what is immoral is what you feel bad after.
— ERNEST HEMINGWAY

goodness

How far that little candle throws his beams!
So shines a good deed in a naughty world.
—WILLIAM SHAKESPEARE

Goodness is easier to recognize than to define.
—W. H. AUDEN

The consequence to the belief that there are no bad people is
that there are no good people.
—MICHAEL LEVINE

Seek not good from without: seek it within yourselves, or you
will never find it.
—EPICTETUS

Jail doesn't teach anyone to do good, nor Siberia, but a man—
yes! A man can teach another man to do good—believe me!
—MAXIM GORKY

Live not as though there were a thousand years ahead of you.
Fate is at your elbow; make yourself good while life and
power are still yours.
—MARCUS AURELIUS

It is one of the beautiful compensations of this life that no one
can sincerely try to help another without helping himself.
—CHARLES DUDLEY WARNER

Do good by stealth and blush to find it fame.
—ALEXANDER POPE

Goodness is the only investment that never fails.
—HENRY DAVID THOREAU

The good hate sin from an innate love of virtue.
—HORACE

Some things must be good in themselves, else there could be
no measure whereby to lay out good and evil.
—BENJAMIN WHICHCOTE

The only fault's with time;
All men become good creatures: but so slow!
—ROBERT BROWNING

It is as hard for the good to suspect evil, as it is for the bad to
suspect good.
—CICERO

Goodness that preaches undoes itself.
—RALPH WALDO EMERSON

While I can crawl upon this planet I think myself obliged to do what good I can, in my narrow domestic spheres, to my fellow creatures, and to wish them all the good I cannot do.
—LORD CHESTERFIELD

The question asked by Confucius centuries ago may be among the most penetrating ever posed: "If we treat those who do bad good, how will we treat those who do good?"
—MICHAEL LEVINE

I did and still do find a serious error in the emphasis of spiritual masters and hagiographers of all faiths on self-denial and austerity as an end in itself, instead of a means. *L'art pour l'art.* We must do the good because it is good, not because it is difficult.
—ADA BATHUNE

She tended to be impatient with that sort of intellectual who, for all his brilliance, has never been able to arrive at the simple conclusion that to be reasonably happy you have to be reasonably good.
—CAROLYN KIZER

It is not enough to do good; one must do it the right way.
— JOHN MORLEY

To talk goodness is not good—only to do it is.
— CHINESE PROVERB

To be proud of virtue is to poison yourself with the antidote.
— BENJAMIN FRANKLIN

If a man wants to be of the greatest possible value to his fellow-creatures, let him begin the long, solitary task of perfecting himself.
— ROBERTSON DAVIES

The soul is stronger that trusts in goodness.
— PHILIP MASSINGER

Good things are not done in a hurry.
— GERMAN PROVERB

Goodness is uneventful. It does not flash, it glows.
— DAVID GRAYSON

few persons have courage enough to appear as good as they really are.

— Julius Charles Hare and
Augustus William Hare

There is so much good in the worst of us and so much bad in the best of us, that it's rather hard to tell which of us ought to reform the rest of us.

— Sign in Springdale,
Connecticut

Don't be too worthwhile. Always keep a few character defects handy. People love to talk about your frailties. If you must be noble, keep it to yourself.

— Edward D. Stone

The whole universe is but the footprint of the divine goodness.

— Dante

Waste no more time arguing what a good man should be. Be one.

— Marcus Aurelius

I'm a believer in God and the ultimate goodness.

— Marian Anderson

Do all the good you can,
By all the means you can,
In all the ways you can,
In all the places you can,
At all the times you can,
To all the people you can,
As long as ever you can.
—JOHN WESLEY

The pleasure of doing good is the only one that will not wear
out.
—CHINESE PROVERB

Be good and leave the rest to heaven.
—WILLIAM COMBE

A glass is good, and a lass is good,
And a pipe to smoke in cold weather;
The world is good, and the people are good,
And we're all good fellows together.
—JOHN O'KEEFE

PART IX

LOVE

Love is filled with strange twists and turns, the vast majority of which cannot be captured in the quotes to follow, much less in this brief introduction.

Gale D. Webbe, an Episcopal priest of great power, once wrote, "The further one grows spiritually, the more and more people one loves and the fewer and fewer one likes." This is inevitable. The further we grow the more we outstrip our peers, whereupon they cease to be our psychospiritual peers. And we can only like our peers, no matter how their number might be declining. Affection is mostly an emotion between equals. On the other hand, we can love virtually anyone if we set our minds to it. But there is little that is warm and bubbly about it. Liking or affection is primarily a feeling; love is primarily a matter of decision and action.

Kurt Vonnegut coined two neologisms that were very useful to me in my practice of psychotherapy: *karass* and *grandfaloon*. By *grandfaloon* he meant an essentially meaningless grouping. The example he gave was Hoosiers—people who just happened to reside in the state of Indiana. He defined a *karass,* to the contrary, as a truly meaningful group. An example I would give is the board of directors of FCE on which Lily and I served for a decade. We directors came from very different walks of life, but we were all leaders of one sort or another, volunteers who were called together by the same passionate commitment to spread a certain vision of community in the world.

Some of the more amusing quotes in this section relate to the difference between friends and relatives or friends and neighbors. This is because families and neighbors are so often types of *grandfaloons*. It was helpful to probably half of my patients when I explained that their families were *grandfaloons*. What a relief it was for them to discover that they were not necessarily obliged to *like* their parents or their siblings! Strangely, this discovery often made it easier for them to *love* these same relatives, to provide for them with care insofar as it was in their power to do so.

The reader may be surprised to note that almost none of the quotes that follow have anything to do with romantic love. This is not an accident. Romantic love is not a virtue; it is a wonderfully pleasant feeling, possibly a purely genetic phenomenon, to facilitate mating, but often misleading and inevitably temporary. There are so many illusions about love that I felt I had no choice in *The Road Less Traveled* but to begin its lengthy section on the subject by proclaiming all the things that genuine love is not. One of them was romantic love. Although I have received over ten thousand letters in response to that book, only one took issue with my proclamation that the bloom of romance always fades; its author was twenty-two years of age.

Then what is genuine love? In that same book I was bold enough to define it as "the will to extend one's self for the purpose of nurturing one's own or another's spiritual growth." But, by God's grace, I had the humility to conclude my discussion of the subject with a subsection entitled "The Mystery of Love," citing some of the ways and reasons that my definition was utterly inadequate.

As noted, Lily and I have been wed for forty years now. That is a long time for a sustained, intimate relationship. I also noted that much of that time was not particularly pleasant.

During it we have gone through all the classical stages of death and dying, as elucidated by Elizabeth Kübler-Ross: denial, anger, bargaining, depression, and acceptance. First we went to great pains to deny that the bloom of our romantic love had faded. When that didn't work and we were faced with our profound differences (which, of course, we perceived as faults) we became angry at each other—and even angrier as we attempted without success to somehow change or "heal" the other. When this strategy failed, we went through a phase of bargaining in which we attempted to develop formulas for working around each other's faults—a phase of negotiation that was without joy. Joyless, we then descended into a lengthy phase of depression wherein each of us seriously wondered, with little hope, whether it was worth it at all. Yet finally and gradually—and almost miraculously—we emerged into a stage where increasingly we began to accept our deep differences of personality as mere differences, often more reflective of virtue than fault. So it was that with complete and heartfelt sincerity I was able to dedicate a recent book "to Lily, fellow journeyman and best friend." We're having a lot of fun together these days.

I do not mean to imply that the longevity of a marriage is necessarily a measure of its health. There are, in fact, marriages in which the partners consistently seem to delight in emotionally attempting to kill each other daily—marriages that survive far more on a strange kind of hate than love. Without attempting to document the fact, however, that is not the way it is between Lily and me. This leaves me with a question: "How is it, then, that our marriage has survived?"

One answer is that we've had a large number of shared

passions ranging from delight in spicy food to delight in travel to foreign lands in order to search for strange and ancient stone monuments. But I believe our most powerful shared passion has been for our own psychospiritual growth. We even attempt to transmit this to others. Indeed, the most common complaint of our staff is: "Oh, no, not the 'G' word again!" Such growth is clearly not everyone's bag. Yet over these years both Lily and I have grown—changed—and, as a result, we've remained interesting to each other. I'm not sure our marriage could have survived without this consistent element of surprise, the element that has continued to keep us "peers," thereby maintaining our mutual affection.

Still, there is something even deeper. As I've so often stated, all the virtues are intertwined, and I believe more powerful than our shared passions have been our shared gifts: compassion, commitment, loyalty, perseverance, and so on. Add all these virtues up, and they can be summed into one: love. Not romantic love but prosaic love. Our marriage has not only survived its vicissitudes but generally overcome them through our prosaic, daily love. But why have we—Lily and I—been given the gift of such love? I do not know. Once again, like all gifts, it is a mystery.

Inexplicable though it may be, there is power in it. Great power. Introducing the previous section, I suggested that this might well be a naturally evil world that has somehow been contaminated by a mysterious infection of goodness, and that the "good bugs" are multiplying. There is a name for this infection: love. The corniest quote I know is that "Love makes the world go around." It is also the only profound truth I know that is not a paradox. Were there some sort of gigantic love vacuum cleaner that could suck all the love out of the earth—all the love that God pours into it and all the love that we humans have for each other—then I fully believe this world would come to a grinding halt in a matter of hours. Yet the reality is that we keep going on, and ever so slowly we seem to be getting a bit better at it. Love is why Dame Julian of Norwich, more than six centuries ago, was enabled to pen the most outrageous proclamation of optimism ever written: "Despite . . . the inevitability of sin, all shall be well, all shall be well, and all manner of thing shall be well."

affection

Affection is created by habit, community of interests, convenience, and the desire of companionship. It is a comfort rather than an exhilaration.
— W. SOMERSET MAUGHAM

'Tis sweet to feel by what fine-spun threads our affections are drawn together.
— LAURENCE STERNE

Praise is well, compliment is well, but affection—that is the last and final and most precious reward that any man can win, whether by character or achievement.
— MARK TWAIN

Do not save your loving speeches
For your friends till they are dead;
Do not write them on their tombstones,
Speak them rather now instead.
— ANNA CUMMINS

The feet carry the body as affection carries the soul.
— ST. CATHERINE OF SIENA

friendship

friendship is a single soul dwelling in two bodies.
— ARISTOTLE

A companion loves some agreeable qualities which a man
may possess, but a friend loves the man himself.
— JAMES BOSWELL

Do not use a hatchet to remove a fly from your friend's
forehead.
— CHINESE PROVERB

friendships, like marriages, are dependent on avoiding the
unforgivable.
— JOHN D. MACDONALD

A man must eat a peck of salt with his friend before he knows
him.
— CERVANTES

It is one of the blessings of old friends that you can afford to
be stupid with them.
— RALPH WALDO EMERSON

We do not so much need the help of our friends as the confidence of their help in need.
— EPICURUS

One's friends are that part of the human race with which one can be human.
— GEORGE SANTAYANA

In politics . . . shared hatreds are almost always the basis of friendships.
— ALEXIS DE TOCQUEVILLE

Your friend is the man who knows all about you, and still likes you.
— ELBERT HUBBARD

When my friends are one-eyed, I look at them in profile.
— JOSEPH JOUBERT

There can be no friendship where there is no freedom. Friendship loves a free air, and will not be fenced up in straight and narrow enclosures.
— WILLIAM PENN

Great souls by instinct to each other turn,
Demand alliance, and in friendship burn.
—JOSEPH ADDISON

If a man should importune me to give a reason why I loved
him, I find it could not otherwise be expressed, than by
making answer: because it was he, because it was I.
—MICHEL DE MONTAIGNE

Friendship either finds or makes equals.
—PUBLILIUS SYRUS

Sooner or later you've heard all your best friends have to say.
Then comes the tolerance of real love.
—NED ROREM

You cannot be friends upon any other terms than upon the
terms of equality.
—WOODROW WILSON

True friendship is a plant of slow growth and must undergo
and withstand the shocks of adversity before it is entitled
to the appellation.
—GEORGE WASHINGTON

Life is nothing without friendship.
— QUINTUS ENNIUS

Friendship's the wine of life.
— EDWARD YOUNG

Greater love hath no man than this, that a man lay down his
life for his friends.
— JOHN 15:13

Friendship cannot live with ceremony, nor without civility.
— LORD HALIFAX

Friendship is the marriage of the soul; and this marriage is
subject to divorce.
— VOLTAIRE

Friendship is not a fruit for enjoyment only, but also an
opportunity for service.
— GREEK PROVERB

The more we love our friends, the less we flatter them; it is by
excusing nothing that pure love shows itself.
— JEAN-BAPTISTE MOLIÈRE

friends are born, not made.
— HENRY ADAMS

You can win more friends with your ears than your mouth.
— ANONYMOUS

Between friends there is no need of justice.
— ARISTOTLE

The bird a nest, the spider a web, man friendship.
— WILLIAM BLAKE

Those who have suffered understand suffering and therefore
extend their hand.
— PATTI SMITH

Being considerate of others will take you and your children
further in life than any college or professional degree.
— MARIAN WRIGHT EDELMAN

I find friendship to be like wine, raw when new, ripened with
age, the true old man's milk and restorative cordial.
— THOMAS JEFFERSON

I have lost friends, some by death . . . others through sheer
inability to cross the street.
— VIRGINIA WOOLF

Friendship closes its eyes rather than see the moon eclipse;
while malice denies that it is ever at the full.
— JULIUS CHARLES HARE AND
AUGUSTUS WILLIAM HARE

The only way to have a friend is to be one.
— RALPH WALDO EMERSON

The easiest kind of relationship for me is with ten thousand
people. The hardest is with one.
— JOAN BAEZ

If I had to choose between betraying my *country* and betraying my *friend,* I hope I should have the guts to betray my
country.
— E. M. FORSTER

Friends are God's apology for relations.
— HUGH KINGSMILL

People's lives change. To keep all your old friends is like
keeping all your old clothes—pretty soon your closet is so
jammed and everything so crushed you can't find anything to wear. Help these friends when they need you;
bless the years and happy times when you meant a lot to
each other, but try *not* to have the guilts if new people
mean more to you now.
— HELEN GURLEY BROWN

The person who tries to live alone will not succeed as a human
being. His heart withers if it does not answer another
heart. His mind shrinks away if he hears only the echos of
his own thoughts and finds no other inspiration.
— PEARL S. BUCK

If I don't have friends, then I ain't got nothin'.
— BILLIE HOLIDAY

Without reciprocal mildness and temperance there can be no
continuance of friendship. Every man will have something to do for his friend, and something to bear within
him.
— OWEN FELLTHAM

A good friend is my nearest relation.
— THOMAS FULLER, M.D.

Real friendship is shown in times of trouble;
prosperity is full of friends.
— EURIPIDES

God gives us our relatives; thank God we can choose our
    friends!
— ETHEL WATTS MUMFORD

No person is your friend who demands your silence, or denies
    your right to grow.
— ALICE WALKER

Each friend represents a world in us, a world possibly not
    born until they arrive, and it is only by this meeting that
    a new world is born.
— ANAÏS NIN

A friend can tell you things you don't want to tell yourself.
— FRANCES WARD WELLER

In time of prosperity friends will be plenty; in time of adver-
    sity not one in twenty.
— ENGLISH PROVERB

It takes two to make a quarrel, but only one to end it.
—SPANISH PROVERB

One loyal friend is worth ten thousand relatives.
—EURIPIDES

Shared joy is double joy, and shared sorrow is half-sorrow.
—SWEDISH PROVERB

Yes'm, old friends is always best, 'less you can catch a new one
that's fit to make an old one out of.
—SARAH ORNE JEWETT

In a world more and more polluted by the lying of politicians and
the illusions of the media, I occasionally crave to hear and
tell the truth. To borrow a beautiful phrase from Friedrich
Nietzsche, I look upon my friend as "the beautiful enemy"
who alone is able to offer me total candor. Friendship is by
its very nature freer of deceit than any other relationship we
can know because it is the bond least affected by striving for
power, physical pleasure, or material profit, most liberated
from any oath of duty or of constancy.
—FRANCINE DU PLESSIX GRAY

Friendship with oneself is all-important, because without it one cannot be friends with anyone else in the world.
— ELEANOR ROOSEVELT

Two may talk together under the same roof for many years, yet never really meet; and two others at first speech are old friends.
— MARY CATHERWOOD

A friend i' the court is better than a penny in the purse.
— WILLIAM SHAKESPEARE

Wishing to be friends is quick work, but friendship is a slow-ripening fruit.
— ARISTOTLE

Old friends are best. King James used to call for his old shoes; they were easiest for his feet.
— JOHN SELDEN

Before borrowing money from a friend decide which you need most.
— AMERICAN PROVERB

friendship admits of difference of character, as love does that
of sex.

— Joseph Roux

A man cannot be said to succeed in this life who does not sat-
isfy one friend.

— Henry David Thoreau

A true friend is one who likes you despite your achievements.

— Arnold Bennett

I like a friend the better for having faults that one can talk
about.

— William Hazlitt

The ornament of a house is the friends who frequent it.

— Ralph Waldo Emerson

The man that hails you Tom or Jack,
And proves by thumps upon your back
How he esteems your merit,
Is such a friend, that one had need
Be very much his friend indeed
To pardon or to bear it.

— William Cowper

I pretend ivry man is honest, and I believe none iv them ar-re.
In that way I keep me friends an' save me money.
— FINLEY PETER DUNNE

I have no trouble with my enemies. But my goddam friends,
. . . they are the ones that keep me walking the floor
nights.
— WARREN G. HARDING

Good friends are good for your health.
— IRWIN SARASON

Fate makes our relatives, choice makes our friends.
— JACQUES DELILLE

In prosperity our friends know us; in adversity we know our
friends.
— CHURTON COLLINS

A friend should bear his friend's infirmities.
— WILLIAM SHAKESPEARE

The shifts of fortune test the reliability of friends.
— CICERO

Think where man's glory most begins and ends
And say my glory was I had such friends.
— WILLIAM BUTLER YEATS

You can hardly make a friend in a year, but you can easily
offend one in an hour.
— CHINESE PROVERB

You can make more friends in two months by becoming more
interested in other people than you can in two years by
trying to get people interested in you.
— DALE CARNEGIE

It is well, when one is judging a friend, to remember that he
is judging you with the same godlike and superior
impartiality.
— ARNOLD BENNETT

There are three faithful friends—an old wife, an old dog, and
ready money.
— BENJAMIN FRANKLIN

Friendship with the wise gets better with time, as a good book
gets better with age.
— THIRUVALLUVAR

A hedge between keeps friendship green.
— ENGLISH PROVERB

A friend that ain't in need is a friend indeed.
— KIN HUBBARD

You can always tell a real friend: When you've made a fool of
yourself he doesn't feel you've done a permanent job.
— LAURENCE J. PETER

I don't like to commit myself about heaven and hell—you see,
I have friends in both places.
— MARK TWAIN

Against a foe I can myself defend,—
But Heaven protect me from a blundering friend!
— D'ARCY W. THOMPSON

Instead of loving your enemies, treat your friends a little better.
— EDGAR HOWE

Love thy neighbor as thyself, but choose your neighborhood.
— LOUISE BEAL

My best friend is the man who in wishing me well wishes it
    for my sake.
                     — ARISTOTLE

No friend's a friend till he shall prove a friend.
                     — BEAUMONT AND FLETCHER

The truth that is suppressed by friends is the readiest weapon
    of the enemy.
                     — ROBERT LOUIS STEVENSON

The condition which high friendship demands is ability to do
    without it.
                     — RALPH WALDO EMERSON

Friendship is honey—but don't eat it all.
                     — MOROCCAN PROVERB

Nine-tenths of the people were created so you would want to
    be with the other tenth.
                     — HORACE WALPOLE

A friend is a speaking acquaintance who also listens.
                     — ARTHUR H. GLASGOW

If we were all given by magic the power to read each other's thoughts, I suppose the first effect would be to dissolve all friendships.
— BERTRAND RUSSELL

The essence of true friendship is to make allowance for another's little lapses.
— DAVID STOREY

A true friend will see you through when others see that you are through.
— LAURENCE J. PETER

Convey thy love to thy friend as an arrow to the mark, to stick there, not as a ball against the wall, to rebound back to thee.
— FRANCIS QUARLES

True friendship comes when silence between two people is comfortable.
— DAVID TYSON GENTRY

In friendship we find nothing false or insincere; everything is straightforward, and springs from the heart.
— CICERO

My wife once said that she likes me to be at home, in my own
study. She doesn't want to talk to me, or to see me, but
she likes to think I'm there. That's exactly how I feel
about the small number of my oldest friends.
—SIR WALTER RALEIGH

friendship is a plant we must often water.
—GERMAN PROVERB

Rather the bite of a friend than the kiss of an enemy.
—SHALOM ALEICHEM

Better a nettle in the side of your friend than his echo.
—RALPH WALDO EMERSON

No man is the whole of himself. His friends are the rest of him.
—PROVERB

I love you not only for what you have made of yourself, but
for what you are making of me.
—ROY CROFT

A friend at one's back is a safe bridge.
—DUTCH SAYING

Every man should have a fair-sized cemetery in which to bury
the faults of his friends.
— HENRY BROOKS ADAMS

A good friend—like a tube of toothpaste—comes through in
a tight squeeze.
— ANONYMOUS

One who looks for a friend without faults will have none.
— HASIDIC SAYING

If the first law of friendship is that it has be cultivated, the second law is to be indulgent when the first law has been
neglected.
— VOLTAIRE

Friendship will not stand the strain of very much good advice
for very long.
— ROBERT LYND

True happiness
Consists not in the multitude of friends,
But in the worth and choice.
— BEN JONSON

We make our friends; we make our enemies; but God makes
our next-door neighbour.
— G. K. CHESTERTON

Friendship is not possible between two women, one of whom
is very well dressed.
— LAURIE COLWIN

Friends do not live in harmony merely, as some say, but in
melody.
— HENRY DAVID THOREAU

My best friend is the one who brings out the best in me.
— HENRY FORD

She's my best friend. I hate her.
— RICHMAL CROMPTON

We have fewer friends than we imagine, but more than we know.
— HUGO VON HOFMANNSTHAL

Of what help is anyone who can only be approached with the
right words?
— ELIZABETH BIBESCO

Sometimes, with luck, we find the kind of true friend, male
or female, that appears only two or three times in a lucky
lifetime, one that will winter us and summer us, grieve,
rejoice, and travel with us.
— BARBARA HOLLAND

Familiarity breeds content.
— ANNA QUINDLEN

Constant use had not worn ragged the fabric of their
friendship.
— DOROTHY PARKER

True friendship is like sound health; the value of it is seldom
known until it be lost.
— CHARLES CALEB COLTON

The friendships which last are those wherein each friend
respects the other's dignity to the point of not really
wanting anything from him.
— CYRIL CONNOLLY

I can trust my friends. . . . These people force me to examine
myself, encourage me to grow.
— CHER

When someone tells you the truth, lets you think for yourself, experience your own emotions, he is treating you as a true equal. As a friend.
— WHITNEY OTTO

I desire so to conduct the affairs of this administration that if at the end, when I come to lay down the reins of power, I have lost every other friend on earth, I shall at least have one friend left, and that friend shall be down inside of me.
— ABRAHAM LINCOLN

I had only one friend, my dog. My wife was mad at me, and I told her a man ought to have at least two friends. She agreed—and bought me another dog.
— PEPPER RODGERS

Don't put your friend in your pocket.
— IRISH PROVERB

A friend of man was he, and thus, he was a friend of God.
— WILSON MACDONALD

I set out to find a friend but couldn't find one; I set out to be a friend, and friends were everywhere.
— ANONYMOUS

Love

If you'd be loved, be worthy to be loved.
— OVID

Love consists in this, that two solitudes protect and border
and salute each other.
— RAINER MARIA RILKE

'Tis better to have loved and lost
Than never to have loved at all.
— ALFRED, LORD TENNYSON

The pounding of your heart in romance and the pounding of
your heart in danger are perhaps the same thing.
— MICHAEL LEVINE

I define love thus: The will to extend one's self for the purpose of nurturing one's own or another's spiritual
growth.
— M. SCOTT PECK

The affirmative of affirmatives is love.
— RALPH WALDO EMERSON

The absolute value of love makes life worth while, and so makes
Man's strange and difficult situation acceptable. Love can-
not save life from death; but it can fulfill life's purpose.
— ARNOLD J. TOYNBEE

Love for the joy of loving, and not for the offerings of someone else's heart.
— MARLENE DIETRICH

Let the dead have the immortality of fame, but the living the
immortality of love.
— RABINDRANATH TAGORE

Love is the subtlest force in the world.
— MAHATMA GANDHI

Love and dignity cannot share the same abode.
— OVID

Few people know what they mean when they say, "I love
you.". . . Well, what does the word *love* mean? It means
total interest. I think the reason very few people really
fall in love with anyone is they're not willing to pay the
price. The price is you have to adjust yourself to them.
— KATHARINE HEPBURN

Love is such a funny thing;
    It's very like a lizard;
It twines itself round the heart
    And penetrates your gizzard.
        —ANONYMOUS

As a romance ends, women don't hurt more than men, just
    differently.
        —MICHAEL LEVINE

It is a curious thought, but it is only when you see people
    looking ridiculous, that you realize just how much you
    love them.
        —AGATHA CHRISTIE

By accident of fortune a man may rule the world for a time,
    but by virtue of love he may rule the world forever.
        —LAO-TZU

We can only learn to love by loving.
        —IRIS MURDOCH

Intellect, in its effort to explain Love, got stuck in the mud
    like an ass. Love alone could explain love and loving.
        —RUMI

We can perhaps learn to prepare for love. We can welcome its coming, we can learn to treasure and cherish it when it comes, but we cannot make it happen. We are elected into love.

— IRENE CLAREMONT DE CASTILLEJO

for one human being to love another: that is perhaps the most difficult of all our tasks, the ultimate, the last test and proof, the work for which all other work is but preparation.

— RAINER MARIA RILKE

Love is the only gold.

— ALFRED, LORD TENNYSON

There is no remedy for love but to love more.

— HENRY DAVID THOREAU

Love is the only force capable of transforming an enemy into a friend.

— MARTIN LUTHER KING JR.

One of the oldest human needs is having someone to wonder where you are when you don't come home at night.

— MARGARET MEAD

When a chap is in love, he will go out in all kinds of weather
to keep an appointment with his beloved. Love can be
demanding, in fact more demanding than law. It has its
own imperatives—think of a mother sitting by the bed-
side of a sick child through the night, impelled only by
love. Nothing is too much trouble for love.
— DESMOND TUTU

Love has nothing to do with what you are expecting to get—
only what you are expecting to give—which is everything. What you will receive in return varies. But it
really has no connection with what you give. You give
because you love and cannot help giving. If you are very
lucky, you may be loved back. That is delicious, but it
does not necessarily happen.
— KATHARINE HEPBURN

Love doesn't have to feel dizzying.
— MICHAEL LEVINE

Who, being loved, is poor?
— OSCAR WILDE

Love knows hidden paths.
— GERMAN PROVERB

The richest love is that which submits to the arbitration of time.

— LAWRENCE DURRELL

Making the decision to have a child—it's momentous. It is to decide forever to have your heart go walking around outside your body.

— ELIZABETH STONE

Love is something like the clouds that were in the sky before the sun came out. You cannot touch the clouds, you know; but you feel the rain and know how glad the flowers and the thirsty earth are to have it after a hot day. You cannot touch love either; but you feel the sweetness that it pours into everything.

— ANNIE SULLIVAN

Love is never abstract. It does not adhere to the universe of the planet or the nation or the institution or the profession, but to the singular sparrows of the street, the lilies of the field, "the least of these my brethren." Love is not, by its own desire, heroic. It is heroic only when compelled to be. It exists by its willingness to be anonymous, humble, and unrewarded.

— WENDELL BERRY

We find love only when we give love to others.
— Douglas M. Lawson

Love talked about can be easily turned aside, but love demon-
strated is irresistible.
— W. Stanley Mooneyham

Love is a power, like money, or steam, or electricity. It is val-
ueless unless you can give something else by means of it.
— Anne Morrow Lindbergh

Life is an attitude. Have a good one.
— Eric L. Lungaard

A life without love, without the presence of the beloved, is
nothing but a mere magic-lantern show. We draw out
slide after slide, swiftly tiring of each, and pushing it
back to make haste for the next.
— Johann Wolfgang von Goethe

Love is that condition in which the happiness of another person is essential to your own.
— Robert A. Heinlein

People need loving the most when they deserve it the least.
— MARY CROWLEY

Love and time are the only two things in this world that cannot be bought, only spent.
— GARY JENNINGS

Love possesses seven hundred wings, and each one extends from the highest heaven to the lowest earth.
— RUMI

Sympathy constitutes friendship; but in love there is a sort of antipathy, or opposing passion. Each strives to be the other, and both together make up one whole.
— SAMUEL TAYLOR COLERIDGE

Among those whom I like or admire, I can find no common denominator, but among those whom I love, I can: all of them make me laugh.
— W. H. AUDEN

Whoso loves
Believes the impossible.
— ELIZABETH BARRETT BROWNING

Love is Nature's second sun.
> —GEORGE CHAPMAN

True love comes quietly, without banners or flashing lights. If
you hear bells, get your ears checked.
> —ERICH SEGAL

Love doesn't just sit there, like a stone, it has to be made, like
bread; remade all the time, made new.
> —URSULA K. LE GUIN

Effort matters in everything, love included. Learning to love
is purposeful work.
> —MICHAEL LEVINE

The Eskimos had fifty-two names for snow because snow was
important to them: there ought to be as many for love.
> —MARGARET ATWOOD

To love and be loved is to feel the sun from both sides.
> —DAVID VISCOTT

RESPECT

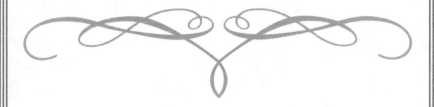

The word respect is derived from the Latin verb, *spicere,* meaning "to look." It is the same word from which we get spectacles, lenses that allow the near blind to not only look but actually see things of importance . . . if we are alert. We are not always so alert.

Many years ago, when I was chief of psychiatry at the U.S. Army Medical Center on Okinawa, I met with a soldier who'd been sent from Vietnam because he had exposed himself over there in a market. Although the episodes had apparently been infrequent, I learned that his history of exhibitionism had been a long one. It seemed to me his exhibitionism was but a symptom of a deep-seated, severe psychiatric disease that made him not responsible for his actions and unfit for military service. Consequently I put him in the hospital to await air evacuation to the United States for medical discharge. He did not strike me as dangerous, so I assigned him to the open ward rather than the locked one. It was a mistake.

At ten the next morning I was called by the director of personnel for the medical center. "Peck, what the hell have you been doing?" he demanded frantically. "One of your patients has been hiding out in a broom closet and exposing himself to every damn cleaning lady in the hospital. I've got thirty women here in my office all screaming at me. Now you get your ass down here and straighten out this mess."

It seemed to me a reasonable request. When I rapidly reached his office I did indeed find thirty Okinawan ladies vociferously expressing their distress in their Japanese dialect. Through the services of the interpreter present, I explained that the man was a known exhibitionist and I was sending him back to the United States as quickly as possible. I said that it had been a mistake for me to have assigned him to an open ward, and I apologized to them profusely. Henceforth, I told them, he would be placed in the locked ward under close observation where, God willing, he would no longer cause them any distress, and I thanked them for their forbearance. Thus mollified, they graciously became understanding. Crisis over.

But the crisis was not over for my soul. Until that moment I hadn't known there were that many cleaning ladies in the hospital. For two years I hadn't noticed them as they quietly went about their daily business. I hadn't even *seen* them. The change in me was not dramatic. I did not go to the trouble to learn Japanese. But for my remaining year on Okinawa I did at least notice these ladies as I passed them in the corridors and now nodded to them in greeting. I paid them that minuscule amount of respect.

This story will ring bells with anyone who has paid the slightest attention to the nature of prejudice. The victims of prejudice are often hard put to say which is worse: the active injustice with which they may be treated or the pervasive, passive disregard they experience whereby they become literally invisible to those in power.

In any case, there is injustice in the world, and several of the quotes to follow take issue with the traditional, sculptural image of justice as a woman holding scales while blindfolded. Properly so. Punishment may be just, but the process of deciding upon it should never be blind. To the contrary, the system of justice that undergirds all that is best in our civilization operates slowly, with seeming inefficiency, precisely because it elaborately takes the time to look at the facts.

As noted, there are evil people in the world, and if we look at them closely we may not like what we see. Moreover, not all of their behavior should be tolerated, and sometimes they need to be locked up. I do not mean to bless the United States in this regard, given the fact that the percentage of its citizens who are incarcerated is the highest in the world. Something is egregiously wrong with our system. Nonetheless, there is no nation on the globe that has found a way to do without its prisons.

But as also noted, there is an inexplicable amount of goodness in the world. Under the aegis of FCE, I have been an active member of perhaps a hundred different community building workshops, mostly comprised of fifty or so participants. We begin these workshops with a story that extols the virtue of respect. Soon the participants begin to behave as if they had never heard the story. But as the process goes on it requires them to look at each other, really look, and by the end of these workshops the story has become embedded in their hearts. Truly looking, they have seen how outrageously good almost all of them are. Among the things these workshops have personally given me is an enormous respect for what I have come to call "the routine heroism of human beings."

One of the most heroic things people can do is to enter deep psychotherapy. Few do so lightly. Most do it in fear and trembling, knowing full well that they are opening themselves to intense scrutiny, that they are rendering themselves psychologically naked, that they will not only be looked at and *seen* by their therapist but also that they will be compelled to truly look at themselves. Most enter therapy assuming they will learn things about themselves that are stupid, sinful, and downright sick. And so they do. If therapy is successful—and often it is not—they will find at least one thing that is "wrong" with themselves. But surprise! To their astonishment, they will almost always find at least several—commonly many—things that are "right," character traits they had taken for granted but which, upon *inspection,* they discover to be noble. In fact, some of these noble traits are ones they had previously thought to be sins, flaws, or weaknesses. As a result, at the conclusion most patients will depart from successful therapy with far greater self-respect than when they first began it.

But please do not think that this business of looking at or regarding another person with respect is necessarily easy or simple. In complex instances—such as are routine not only in courts of law but also between husbands and wives or parents and children—understanding is required. That is why I have listed it as one of the component virtues of respect.

Understanding is a concept almost everyone thinks he understands. Seldom is this the case. Consider the literal meaning of the word: to stand under. To understand someone else in any depth whatsoever you must be willing to stand under that person—that is, at least temporarily, to put her in authority over you.

Hey, wait a minute! I'm a man. Do you mean I should put a woman in authority over me? Specifically, I'm a heterosexual man. Am I to place a gay person in the position of being my boss? I'm a parent; should I hand over the reins to my children? I'm a successful man; are you asking me to look up to a homeless person?

Yes, these are exactly the kinds of things I am asking you to do . . . temporarily. I'm not telling you to become a woman, a homosexual, a child, or a homeless person (even though you might have a sneaking desire to do so!). But I am telling you to take the time and mental effort to wonder what it's like to be a woman, to entertain the possibility of being gay, to remember the burdens of being a child, to place yourself in the shoes of someone who is homeless. In the end I'm not asking you to obey them. But at the very least I am asking you to take the time to seriously look at the possibility that that woman or gay or child or homeless person might well, in fact, be wiser than you. Think about it. Really think about it.

It requires some stretching, doesn't it? Some extension of yourself, some mental effort? But that's just what I said a little way back about love, and why should understanding and respect be any different? When genuine, these are not fuzzy feelings; they are mostly work. But they are a kind of work more likely to pay off handsomely than any garage you ever cleaned or any dollar you ever made.

Brotherhood

Heaven is my Father, the earth my mother, and even a tiny creature such as myself finds an intimate place in their midst. In everything that moves through the universe, I see my own body, and in everything that governs the universe, my own soul. All men are my brethren, and all things my companions.
— CHANG TSAI

The opportunity to practice brotherhood presents itself every time you meet a human being.
— JANE WYMAN

While there is a lower class I am in it, while there is a criminal element I am of it; while there is a soul in prison, I am not free.
— EUGENE V. DEBS

We seek not the worldwide victory of one nation or system, but a worldwide victory of men.
— JOHN F. KENNEDY

The universal brotherhood of man is our most precious possession, what there is of it.
— MARK TWAIN

Grant stood by me when I was crazy, and I stood by him
when he was drunk, and now we stand by each other.
— WILLIAM TECUMSEH SHERMAN

It is easier to love humanity as a whole than to love one's
neighbor.
— ERIC HOFFER

I remember one night at Muzdalifah . . . I lay awake amid
sleeping Muslim brothers and I learned that pilgrims
from every land—every color and class and rank—all
snored in the same language.
— MALCOLM X

We must not only affirm the brotherhood of man; we must
live by it.
— HENRY CODMAN POTTER

It would be much better to have the one week in fifty-two
dedicated to hate, a week when we would all be able to
get the hate out of our systems, treat one another as badly
as we know how, and then observe the remaining fifty-
one weeks as Brotherhood Weeks.
— RABBI SAMUEL PRICE

Do you love your Creator? Love your fellow-beings first.
— MUHAMMAD

My country is the world; my countrymen are mankind.
— WILLIAM LLOYD GARRISON

There is no escape—man drags man down, or man lifts man up.
— BOOKER T. WASHINGTON

We must strengthen, defend, preserve and comfort each other. We must love one another. We must bear one another's burdens. We must not look only on our things, but also on the things of our brethren. We must rejoice together, mourn together, labor and suffer together.
— JOHN WINTHROP

Brotherhood doesn't come in a package. It is not a commodity to be taken down from the shelf with one hand—it is an accomplishment of soul-searching prayer and perseverance.
— OVETA CULP HOBBY

The answer to the question, "Am I my brother's keeper?" must always be "No—! I am my brother's brother."
— DR. PAUL KLAPPER

However dark the prospects, however intractable the opposition, however devious and mendacious the diplomacy of our opponents, we ourselves have to carry so clear and intense a picture of our common humanity that we see the brother beneath the enemy and snatch at every opportunity to break through to his reason and his conscience, and, indeed, his enlightened self-interest.
— ADLAI E. STEVENSON

Perhaps the clearest and deepest meaning of brotherhood is the ability to imagine yourself in the other person's position, and then treat that person as if you were him. This form of brotherhood takes a lot of imagination, a great deal of sympathy, and a tremendous amount of understanding.
— OBERT C. TANNER

If you really believe in the brotherhood of man, and you want to come into its fold, you've got to let everyone else in too.
— OSCAR HAMMERSTEIN

I have a dream that one day on the red hills of Georgia the sons of former slaves and the sons of former slaveowners will be able to sit down together at the table of brotherhood.
— MARTIN LUTHER KING JR.

It is easy enough to be friendly to one's friends. But to befriend the one who regards himself as your enemy is the quintessence of true religion. The other is mere business.

— MAHATMA GANDHI

Our most basic common link is that we all inhabit this planet. We all breathe the same air. We all cherish our children's future. And we are all mortal.

— JOHN F. KENNEDY

We are each of us angels with only one wing. And we can only fly embracing each other.

— LUCIANO DE CRESCENZO

Humanitarianism

Do not give, as many rich men do, like a hen that lays her egg and then cackles.

— HENRY WARD BEECHER

If charity cost no money and benevolence caused no heartache, the world would be full of philanthropists.

— YIDDISH PROVERB

It is better to light a candle than to curse the darkness.
— CHINESE PROVERB

He that gives his heart will not deny his money.
— THOMAS FULLER, M.D.

A decent provision for the poor is the true test of civilization.
— SAMUEL JOHNSON

Philanthropy is commendable, but it must not cause the philanthropist to overlook the circumstances of economic
injustice which make philanthropy necessary.
— MARTIN LUTHER KING JR.

Benevolence doesn't consist in those who are prosperous pity-
ing and helping those who are not. Benevolence consists
in fellow feeling that puts you upon actually the same
level with the fellow who suffers.
— WOODROW WILSON

Sow good services; sweet remembrances will grow from
them.
— MADAME DE STAEL

justice

Justice is truth in action.
— JOSEPH JOUBERT

Justice is a contract of expediency, entered upon to prevent man harming or being harmed.
— EPICURUS

Justice will not condemn even the Devil himself wrongfully.
— THOMAS FULLER, M.D.

A man should not act as a judge either for someone he loves or for someone he hates. For no man can see the guilt of someone he loves or the good qualities in someone he hates.
— TALMUD

Though justice moves slowly, it seldom fails to overtake the wicked.
— HORACE

I never promised you a rose garden. I never promised you perfect justice.
— HANNAH GREEN

Justice should remove the bandage from her eyes long enough
to distinguish between the vicious and the unfortunate.
— ROBERT G. INGERSOLL

Justice has nothing to do with expediency. It has nothing to do
with any temporary standard whatever. It is rooted and
grounded in the fundamental instincts of humanity.
— WOODROW WILSON

It is better to risk saving a guilty man than to condemn an
innocent one.
— VOLTAIRE

It is impossible to be just if one is not generous.
— JOSEPH ROUX

Justice without force is powerless; force without justice is
tyrannical.
— BLAISE PASCAL

Justice may wink a while, but see at last.
— THOMAS MIDDLETON

Justice delayed is democracy denied.
— ROBERT F. KENNEDY

If you wish to know what justice is, let injustice pursue you.
— EUGENIO MARIA DE HOSTOS

There is no happiness, there is no liberty, there is no enjoyment of life, unless a man can say, when he rises in the
morning, I shall be subject to the decision of no unwise
judge today.
— DANIEL WEBSTER

Truth is justice's handmaid, freedom is its child, peace is its
companion, safety walks in its steps, victory follows in its
train.
— SYDNEY SMITH

An unrectified case of injustice has a terrible way of lingering,
restlessly, in the social atmosphere like an unfinished
question.
— MARY MCCARTHY

Judging from the main portions of the history of the world, so
far, justice is always in jeopardy.
— WALT WHITMAN

He injures the good who spares the bad.
— PUBLILIUS SYRUS

It is better to protest than to accept injustice.
— ROSA PARKS

Sparing justice feeds iniquity.
— WILLIAM SHAKESPEARE

I shall temper . . . justice with mercy.
— JOHN MILTON

No man can be just who is not free.
— WOODROW WILSON

To withdraw ourselves from the law of the strong, we have
found ourselves obliged to submit to justice. Justice or
might, we must choose between these two masters: so
little are we made to be free.
— LUC DE VAUVENARGUES

Justice is only possible when to every man belongs the power
to resist and claim redress for wrongs.
— ROBERT BRIFFAULT

Justice is so subtle a thing, to interpret it one has only need of a heart.
— JOSE GARCIA OLIVER

If we are to keep our democracy, there must be one commandment: Thou shalt not ration justice.
— LEARNED HAND

Be just before you're generous.
— RICHARD BRINSLEY SHERIDAN

Man's capacity for justice makes democracy possible; but man's inclination to injustice makes democracy necessary.
— REINHOLD NIEBUHR

Many of the ugly pages of American history have been obscured and forgotten. . . . America owes a debt of justice which it has only begun to pay. If it loses the will to finish or slackens in its determination, history will recall its crimes and the country that would be great will lack the most indispensable element of greatness—justice.
— MARTIN LUTHER KING JR.

Justice cannot be for one side alone, but must be for both.
— ELEANOR ROOSEVELT

It is still in the lap of the gods whether a society can succeed
which is based on "civil liberties and human rights" conceived as I have tried to describe them; but of one thing
at least we may be sure: The alternatives that have so far
appeared have been immeasurably worse.
—LEARNED HAND

Justice is the end of government. It is the end of civil society.
It ever has been and ever will be pursued until it be
obtained, or until liberty be lost in the pursuit.
—ALEXANDER HAMILTON

self-respect

Never bend your head. Always hold it high. Look the world
straight in the eye.
—HELEN KELLER

It is difficult to make a man miserable while he feels worthy
of himself and claims kindred to the great God who
made him.
—ABRAHAM LINCOLN

No one can make you feel inferior without your consent.
— ELEANOR ROOSEVELT

So much is a man worth as he esteems himself.
— RABELAIS

Have respect for your species. . . . You are a man; do not dishonour mankind.
— JEAN-JACQUES ROUSSEAU

Don't compromise yourself. You are all you've got.
— JANIS JOPLIN

Self-respect—the secure feeling that no one, as yet, is suspicious.
— H. L. MENCKEN

I have an everyday religion that works for me. Love yourself first and everything else falls into line. You really have to love yourself to get anything done in this world.
— LUCILLE BALL

Learn what you are, and be such.
— PINDAR

To be nobody but yourself—in a world which is doing its best, night and day, to make you everybody else—means to fight the hardest battle which any human being can fight, and never stop fighting.

— E. E. CUMMINGS

Self-respect will keep a man from being abject when he is in the power of enemies, and will enable him to feel that he may be in the right when the world is against him.

— BERTRAND RUSSELL

I firmly believe that if you follow a path that interests you, not to the exclusion of love, sensitivity, and cooperation with others, but with the strength of conviction that you can move others by your own efforts, and do not make success of failure the criteria by which you live, the chances are you'll be a person worthy of your own respect.

— NEIL SIMON

An individual's self-concept is the core of his personality. It affects every aspect of human behavior; the ability to learn, the capacity to grow and change, the choice of friends, mates and careers. It is no exaggeration to say that a strong, positive self-image is the best possible preparation for success in life.

— DR. JOYCE BROTHERS

A man cannot be comfortable without his own approval.
—MARK TWAIN

Remember always that you have not only the right to be an
individual, you have an obligation to be one. You cannot
make any useful contribution in life unless you do this.
—ELEANOR ROOSEVELT

To have that sense of one's intrinsic worth which constitutes
self-respect is potentially to have everything.
—JOAN DIDION

Once you get rid of the idea that you must please other people
before you please yourself, and you begin to follow your
own instincts—only then can you be successful. You become more satisfied, and when you are other people tend
to be satisfied by what you do.
—RAQUEL WELCH

Even a slug is a star if it dares to be its horned and slimy self.
—JOHN HARGRAVE

He that respects himself is safe from others, he wears a coat of
mail that none can pierce.
—HENRY WADSWORTH LONGFELLOW

tolerance

I do not agree with a word that you say, but I will defend to
the death your right to say it.
— VOLTAIRE

If we cannot end our differences, at least we can help make
the world safe for diversity.
— JOHN F. KENNEDY

It is a good thing to demand liberty for ourselves and for those
who agree with us, but it is a better thing and a rarer
thing to give liberty to others who do not agree with us.
— FRANKLIN D. ROOSEVELT

So long as a man rides his hobbyhorse peaceably and quietly
along the King's highway, and neither compels you or
me to get up behind him,—pray, Sir, what have either
you or I to do with it?
— LAURENCE STERNE

By burning Luther's books you may rid your bookshelves of
him, but you will not rid men's minds of him.
— ERASMUS

Pray you use your freedom,
And so far as you please, allow me mine.
To hear you only; not to be compelled
To take your moral potions.
— PHILIP MASSINGER

Live and let live.
— PROVERB

Tolerance is only complacence when it makes no distinction
between right and wrong.
— SARAH PATTON BOYLE

It is the will and command of God that . . . a permission of the
paganish, Jewish, Turkish, or anti-Christian consciences
and worships be granted to all men in all nations and
countries; and they are only to be fought against with
that sword which is only (in soul matters) able to con-
quer, to wit, the sword of God's spirit, the Word of God.
— ROGER WILLIAMS

I tolerate with the utmost latitude the right of others to differ from me in opinion without imputing to them crim-
inality. I know too well the weakness and uncertainty of
human reason to wonder at its different results.
— THOMAS JEFFERSON

Toleration . . . is the greatest gift of the mind; it requires the
same effort of the brain that it takes to balance oneself on
a bicycle.
— HELEN KELLER

Differing from a man in doctrine was no reason why you
should pull his house about his ears.
— SAMUEL JOHNSON

If you will please people, you must please them in their own
way; and as you cannot make them what they should be,
you must take them as they are.
— LORD CHESTERFIELD

In a republic we must learn to combine intensity of conviction
with a broad tolerance of difference of conviction. Wide
differences of opinion in matters of religious, political,
and social belief must exist if conscience and intellect
alike are not to be stunted.
— THEODORE ROOSEVELT

Laws alone cannot secure freedom of expression; in order that
every man present his views without penalty there must
be a spirit of tolerance in the entire population.
— ALBERT EINSTEIN

The first thing to learn in intercourse with others is non-interference with their own peculiar ways of being happy, provided those ways do not assume to interfere by violence with ours.

—WILLIAM JAMES

In the practice of tolerance, one's enemy is the best teacher.

—FOURTEENTH DALAI LAMA

There is a difference between justice and consideration in one's relations to one's fellow men. It is the function of justice not to do wrong to one's fellow men; of considerateness, not to wound their feelings.

—CICERO

There is no such thing as justice in the abstract; it is merely a compact between men.

—EPICURUS

The longer I live, the larger allowances I make for human infirmities.

—JOHN WESLEY

I hate people who are intolerant.

—LAURENCE J. PETER

Tolerance is the positive and cordial effort to understand another's beliefs, practices, and habits without necessarily
sharing or accepting them.
— JOSHUA LIEBMAN

Tolerance implies no lack of commitment to one's own beliefs.
Rather it condemns the oppression or persecution of others.
— JOHN F. KENNEDY

The full circle of spiritual truth will be completed only when
we realize that, but for a destiny not fully understood, we
might actually have been born in the other person's faith.
— MARCUS BACH

understanding

Do naught thou dost not understand.
— PYTHAGORAS

Understanding is the beginning of approving.
— ANDRÉ GIDE

A moment's insight is sometimes worth a life's experience.
—OLIVER WENDELL HOLMES SR.

To understand is to forgive, even oneself.
—ALEXANDER CHASE

Ten lands are sooner known than one man.
—YIDDISH PROVERB

It is a profound philosophy to sound the depths of feeling and distinguish traits of character. Men must be studied as deeply as books.
—BALTASAR GRACIÁN

Believe nothing, O monks, merely because you have been told it . . . or because it is traditional, or because you yourselves have imagined it. Do not believe what your teacher tells you merely out of respect for the teacher. But whatsoever, after due examination and analysis, you find to be conducive to the good, the benefit, the welfare of all beings— that doctrine believe and cling to, and take it as your guide.
—BUDDHA

If you would judge, understand.
—SENECA

It is easier to know (and understand) men in general than one man in particular.

— La Rochefoucauld

The wave is ignorant of the true nature of the sea: how can the temporal comprehend the eternal?

— Sa'ib of Tabriz

I want, by understanding myself, to understand others. I want to be all that I am capable of becoming.

— Katherine Mansfield

There is no way of seeing things without first taking leave of them.

— Antonio Machado

The motto should not be: Forgive one another; rather, Understand one another.

— Emma Goldman

The growth of understanding follows an ascending spiral rather than a straight line.

— Joanna Field

The brain is like a muscle. When we think well, we feel good.
Understanding is a kind of ecstasy.
— CARL SAGAN

Grant that we may not so much seek to be understood as to
understand.
— ST. FRANCIS OF ASSISI

I firmly believe kids don't want your understanding. They
want your trust, your compassion, your blinding love,
and your car keys, but try to understand them and you're
in big trouble.
— ERMA BOMBECK

All the glory of greatness has no lustre for people who are in
search of understanding.
— BLAISE PASCAL

Great understanding is broad and unhurried; little understanding is cramped and busy.
— CHUANG-TZU

Each of us really understands in others only those feelings he
is capable of producing himself.
— ANDRÉ GIDE

Respect

Respect a man, he will do the more.
— JAMES HOWELL

Without feelings of respect, what is there to distinguish men
from beasts?
— CONFUCIUS

If you have some respect for people as they are, you can be
more effective in helping them to become better than
they are.
— JOHN W. GARDNER

We have always felt the sympathy of the world, but we would
prefer the respect of the world to sympathy without
respect.
— ANWAR SADAT

He that respects not is not respected.
— GEORGE HERBERT

The respect that is only bought by gold is not worth much.
— FRANCES ELLEN WATKINS HARPER

We must respect everyone who lives on this earth, be he French or foreigner. We must treat him as a brother so long as he respects our freedom, our personality, and our dignity.

— Habib ibn Ali Bourguiba

To honor an old man is showing respect to God.

— Muhammad

I had to fight hard against loneliness, abuse, and the knowledge that any mistake I made would be magnified because I was the only black man out there. Many people resented my impatience and honesty, but I never cared about acceptance as much as I cared about respect.

— Jackie Robinson

I am not going to respect . . . gray hairs unless there is wisdom beneath them.

— Mohammed Ali Jinna

Man does not live by bread alone. Many prefer self-respect to food.

— Mahatma Gandhi

PART XI

STRENGTH

I have suggested that humanity is ever so slowly (maybe not so slowly, when you think about it) evolving into greater goodness, toward its true destiny of humaneness. The way we use the word *strength* mirrors this evolution. One or two thousand years ago when we spoke of a person's strength, we generally meant his physical strength: his capacity by virtue of pure musculature to beat other people up and hence rule over them or take their wives. Today when we talk of a person's strength we are usually doing so in purely psychological terms, specifically referring to his or her "strength of character."

We have also evolved from a primarily agricultural society (where brute, physical strength was often a virtue) into a primarily industrial one. This has further been an evolution into organizational complexity. A mere hundred years ago the vast majority of people worked on small family farms. Today they work for gigantic businesses where the greater skills required are organizational ones. The capacity to lift heavy objects is of no consequence. The capacity to collaborate (labor together) and cooperate may be everything.

One might think the best position from which to assess a person's character would be the psychiatrist's chair. On occasion that is true. But my predominant experience has been the better (albeit often more painful) position has been that of an executive's chair. Just as there are evil people in contradistinction to good ones, so there are weak people as well as strong ones. The weak ones may not be evil, but they are the bane of an executive's existence. What characterizes them the most is their incapacity or unwillingness to cooperate and collaborate.

To put the matter simply, you just can't count on them.

The majority of my organizational experience has been working with FCE, which is primarily a volunteer organization. A sense of duty is far more important in a volunteer than a paid employee. The employee often comes to work in the morning only because she may not get paid if she doesn't. The volunteer comes to work purely because she said she would. She is, in fact, under no other obligation to keep her commitments other than her duty or obligation to herself. This is why it is frequently difficult to find dependable volunteers. Mary Ann Schmidt, the late, long-term chairman of the board of FCE, was wont to speak of the backbone of the organization, its "people strength," by saying, "They keep showing up."

Most volunteers do not work for charitable organizations. The most common volunteer role is that of parent, and it is work indeed. The good parent is he or she who keeps "showing up." Think of the sad child who cannot count upon his parents to pick him up after school or soccer practice! It is the job of the parent to be there.

Until they were well grown, Lily and I used to think of ourselves as our children's servants. This was not demeaning. It is important to remember that the servant is in a position of power. She is not a slave. A slave is someone who does whatever her master *wants.* A servant is someone who does whatever the master *needs,* and it is she who decides what this might be. Wherever the decision making resides, that's where the power is. Lily and I hope that we did almost everything our children needed. If we had done everything they wanted, however, we would not have served them well.

So, although parents are properly their children's servants, they are also leaders. And the decisions they must make about what their children need are often as agonizingly complex as any that are made by the most mighty business executives.

Truly good parents and truly good executives have much in common, but one virtue seems to me preeminent: the desire to empower. Sadly, many lack it. Huge numbers of parents unconsciously want to keep their children as children, even to the point of "infantilizing" them. Similarly, the last thing most business executives like to think about is handing over the reins. Yet the deepest desire of great parents and executives is the opposite: It is to see that their children and subordinates become strong—even stronger and more powerful than they themselves. They know that the ultimate purpose of power, like wealth, is to give it away. Their desire to give it away is so strong they often find they must restrain themselves. Rushing to hand over the reins may be a serious abdication. But slowly and surely they will nurture their children and subordinates into ever-increasing strength, not only so that they themselves can gracefully retire, not only so that they can rejoice in the potency of their progeny, but because it is the best way they can serve the world. This is why the famed management consultant, John K. Greenleaf, referring to such women and men, coined the term "servant-leadership."

So we are yet once again back to paradox. We are accustomed to thinking of the servant as the one who obeys and the leader as the one who commands, the leader as strong and the servant as weak. It is no accident that in this book obedience is counted as one of the component virtues of strength. The man who can only lead is weakened by his compulsion to lead.

Similarly, however, the woman who can only obey is

weakened by her compulsion to obedience. Thus this section on strength also includes the virtue of moderation. Obedience carried to an extreme, like the other virtues, is a sin. But such moderation is not always cheaply purchased. Consider military life where obedience is at a premium. It is illegal to fail to obey a command of a superior officer. Doing so can put you in prison. At the same time, the poor soldier is instructed that it is also illegal to obey an illegal order, and that by doing so he can also be put in prison. A dilemma, is it not?

How to resolve such a dilemma? In the heat of battle (or parenthood) the soldier does not have law books within reach, much less the availability of legal counsel. The answer, of course, is that ultimately he is supposed to obey his own conscience, even on the spur of the moment. Fine, but from whence comes his conscience? Psychologists have developed several theories about the matter, but they are only theories at best. The fact is, we don't know the origins of conscience.

Despite my identity as a psychiatrist, there is a theological explanation of the conscience that bears more weight for me than "developmental" theories. Theologians have noted that, regardless of their background, all children seem to have an innate sense of fairness. They are not necessarily likely to apply this sense to their own behavior toward others, but they are instinctively quick to apply it to themselves whenever they feel aggrieved. "But it's not *fair!*" they will exclaim in natural self-defense.

So the theologians propose that we are all born with a conscience as a gift from God. That this is so has even been used as one of the arguments for the existence of God. Nonetheless, although I believe this proposal, it still seems to me to beg some questions. It is rather easy to say, "Our conscience is the voice of God bred into us, and our strength lies in our capacity to obey this voice." The voice does seem to differ from person to person, however, and our inclination to obey it is vastly different. On the one hand, in His or Her love of diversity, God may not give each of us exactly the same conscience. On the other, our free will seems to make a considerable difference.

So let me say this, extreme or mystical though it might seem: Our strength of character ultimately resides in our willingness to obey not our earthly superiors but the voice of God that resides within us. However, it is also our free will to decide who God is and who God isn't.

Talk about strength and power! In this sense it is not so much God who creates us, as we poor soldiers who create God. It is a rather frightening notion, which I offer here in part to prepare us for the next and final section on the essence of Wisdom.

What kind of God do we want most to create? A God of dominance or a God of service? Most people, perhaps, have opted for the image of a God of dominance who not only created everything but continues to control it all, fairly or unfairly, with omnipotent albeit mysterious power. St. Paul, however, enamored by the concept that God was actually willing to die a seemingly powerless death upon a cross for us, clearly decided for a God of service. He then decided to be obedient to that God, and gave us the ultimately paradoxical teaching, "In weakness there is strength."

DUTY

For unto whomsoever much is given, of him shall be much
   required.
   —LUKE 12:48

No man can always be right. So the struggle is to do one's best;
   to keep the brain and conscience clear; never to be
   swayed by unworthy motives or inconsequential reasons,
   but to strive to unearth the basic factors involved and
   then do one's duty.
   —DWIGHT D. EISENHOWER

If a sense of duty tortures a man, it also enables him to achieve
   prodigies.
   —H. L. MENCKEN

Do your duty, and leave the rest to the gods.
   —PIERRE CORNEILLE

I long to accomplish a great and noble task, but it is my chief
   duty to accomplish small tasks as if they were great and
   noble.
   —HELEN KELLER

Without duty, life is soft and boneless; it cannot hold itself together.

— Joseph Joubert

Duties are not performed for duty's sake, but because their neglect would make the man uncomfortable. A man performs but one duty—the duty of contenting his spirit, the duty of making himself agreeable to himself.

— Mark Twain

There is no growth except in the fulfillment of obligations.

— Antoine de Saint-Exupéry

There is no duty we so much underrate as the duty of being happy.

— Robert Louis Stevenson

Obligation may be stretched till it is no better than a brand of slavery stamped on us when we were too young to know its meaning.

— George Eliot

Never step over one duty to perform another.

— English proverb

To live without duties is obscene.
—RALPH WALDO EMERSON

Duty is lighter than a feather, but heavier than a mountain.
—MEIJI TENNO

The last pleasure in life is the sense of discharging our duty.
—WILLIAM HAZLITT

We need to restore the full meaning of that old word, duty. It
is the other side of rights.
—PEARL S. BUCK

We cannot hope to scale great moral heights by ignoring petty
obligations.
—AGNES REPPLIER

You are a member of the British royal family. We are never
tired, and we all *love* hospitals.
—QUEEN MARY

When you have a number of disagreeable duties to perform,
always do the most disagreeable first.
—JOSIAH QUINCY

I declare my belief that it is not your duty to do anything that
is not to your own interest. Whenever it is unquestionably your duty to do a thing, then it will benefit you to
perform that duty.
—EDGAR WATSON HOWE

A sense of duty is moral glue, constantly subject to stress.
—WILLIAM SAFIRE

Man's responsibility increases as that of the gods decreases.
—ANDRÉ GIDE

Our main business is not to see what lies dimly at a distance,
but to do what lies clearly at hand.
—THOMAS CARLYLE

Reason shows us our duty; he who can make us love our duty
is more powerful than reason itself.
—STANISLAUS LESZCYNSKI

My great wish is to go on in a strict but silent performance of
my duty; to avoid attracting notice, and to keep my name
out of newspapers.
—THOMAS JEFFERSON

Duty cannot exist without faith.
— Benjamin Disraeli

When Elijah was waiting with impatience for the divine Presence in the wilderness, he found that God was not clothed in the whirlwind or in the earthquake, but that He was in the still small voice of duty.
— Charles E. Garman

In duty the individual finds his liberation; liberation from dependence on mere natural impulse.
— G. W. F. Hegel

The Church of God has to be the salt and light of the world. We are the hope of the hopeless, through the power of God. We must transfigure a situation of hate and suspicion, of brokenness and separation, of fear and bitterness. We have no option. We are servant to the God who reigns and cares.
— Desmond Tutu

In practice it is seldom very hard to do one's duty when one knows what it is, but it is sometimes exceedingly difficult to find this out.
— Samuel Butler

You will always find those who think they know what is your
duty better than you know it.
— RALPH WALDO EMERSON

The reward of one duty done is the power to fulfill another.
— GEORGE ELIOT

moderation

There is a proper measure in all things, certain limits beyond
which and short of which right is not to be found.
— HORACE

Moderation is the silken string running though the pearl
chain of all virtues.
— JOSEPH HALL

Only the intelligent can understand what is obvious and what
is concealed. Strength may be good or it may be evil. The
same is true of weakness. The ideal is moderation. . . .
Purify the heart, that is all.
— CHOU-TUN-I

This only grant me, that my means may lie
Too low for envy, for contempt too high.
— ABRAHAM COWLEY

I like to operate like a submarine on sonar. When I am pick-
ing up noise from both the left and right, I know my
course is correct.
— GUSTAVO DIAZ ORDAZ

Let's not get too full of ourselves. Let's leave space for God to
come into the room.
— QUINCY JONES

We never repent of having eaten too little.
— THOMAS JEFFERSON

Stretch the bow to the very full,
And you will wish you had stopped in time.
— LAO-TZU

Without a sense of proportion there can be neither good taste
nor genuine intelligence, nor perhaps moral integrity.
— ERIC HOFFER

obedience

Every great person has first learned how to obey, whom to
obey, and when to obey.
—William Ward

The man who does something under orders is not unhappy;
he is unhappy who does something against his will.
—Seneca

We ought to obey God rather than man.
—Acts 5:29

This free will business is a bit terrifying anyway. It's almost
pleasanter to obey, and make the most of it.
—Ugo Betti

Woe to him that claims obedience when it is not due; woe to
him that refuses when it is!
—Thomas Carlyle

Learn to obey before you command.
—Solon

"She still seems to me in her own way a person born to com-
mand," said Luce. . . .
"I wonder if anyone is born to obey," said Isabel.
"That may be why people command rather badly, that they
have no suitable material to work on."
— IVY COMPTON-BURNETT

Obey what is revealed you from your Lord. God is aware of
all you do. And put your trust in Him, for He is your
guardian and trustee.
— QUR'AN

You cannot be a true man until you learn to obey.
— ROBERT E. LEE

responsibility

To some degree, you control your life by controlling your
time.
— MICHAEL LEVINE

The ability to accept responsibility is the measure of the man.
— ROY L. SMITH

Our privileges can be no greater than our obligations. The protection of our rights can endure no longer than the performance of our responsibilities.
— JOHN F. KENNEDY

To be a man is, precisely, to be responsible.
— ANTOINE DE SAINT-EXUPÉRY

You must create your own world. I am responsible for my world.
— LOUISE NEVELSON

Man must cease attributing his problems to his environment, and learn again to exercise his will—his personal responsibility in the realm of faith and morals.
— ALBERT SCHWEITZER

It is quite easy to shout slogans, to sign manifestos, but it is quite a different matter to build, manage, command, spend days and nights seeking the solution of problems.
— PATRICE LUMUMBA

Man must now assume the responsibility for his world. He can no longer shove it off on religious power.
— HARVEY COX

Somewhere along the line of development we discover what we really are, and then we make our real decision for which we are responsible. Make that decision primarily for yourself, because you can never really live anyone else's life, not even your own child's. The influence you exert is through your own life and what you become yourself.

— ELEANOR ROOSEVELT

Every man must carry his own sack to the mill.

— ITALIAN PROVERB

While living I want to live well. I know I have to die sometime, but even if the heavens were to fall on me, I want to do what is right. There is one God looking down on us all. We are all children of the one God. God is listening to me. The sun, the darkness, the winds, are listening to what we now say.

— GERONIMO

Responsibility, n. A detachable burden easily shifted to the shoulders of God, Fate, Fortune, Luck or one's neighbor. In the days of astrology it was customary to unload it upon a star.

— AMBROSE BIERCE

Even though a person may work for a living, they must also devote time and effort to the care of their home and family. This is the true measure of an industrious person.
— CLIVE BARLOW

Few things help an individual more than to place responsibility upon him, and to let him know that you trust him.
— BOOKER T. WASHINGTON

A bad workman always blames his tools.
— PROVERB

. . . Each man the architect of his own fate.
— APPIUS CAECUS

It often happens that I wake at night and begin to think about a serious problem and decide I must tell the Pope about it. Then I wake up completely and remember I am the Pope.
— POPE JOHN XXIII

Accuse not Nature, she hath done her part;
Do thou but thine.
— JOHN MILTON

Responsibility is the thing people dread most of all. Yet it is the only thing in the world that develops us, gives us manhood or womanhood fibre.
— FRANK CRANE

We often have to put up with most from those on whom we most depend.
— BALTASAR GRACIÁN

We can believe what we choose. We are answerable for what we choose to believe.
— CARDINAL NEWMAN

The salvation of mankind lies only in making everything the concern of all.
— ALEKSANDR SOLZHENITSYN

Responsibilities gravitate to the person who can shoulder them.
— ELBERT HUBBARD

Life for most of us is full of steep stairs to go puffing up and, later, of shaky stairs to totter down; and very early in the history of stairs must have come the invention of banisters.
— LOUIS KRONENBERGER

If each one sweeps before his own door, the whole street is
clean.
— YIDDISH PROVERB

self-discipline

Would you live with ease, do what you ought, and not what
you please.
— BENJAMIN FRANKLIN

He who requires much from himself and little from others,
will keep himself from being the object of resentment.
— CONFUCIUS

Do not consider painful what is good for you.
— EURIPIDES

If men live decently it is because discipline saves their very
lives for them.
— SOPHOCLES

Submit to the rule you laid down.
— ENGLISH PROVERB

What it lies in our power to do, it lies in our power not to do.
— ARISTOTLE

When things are steep, remember to stay level-headed.
— HORACE

freedom is not procured by a full enjoyment of what is desired, but by controlling the desire.
— EPICTETUS

No one who cannot limit himself has ever been able to write.
— NICHOLAS BOILEAU

for better or worse, man is the tool-using animal, and as such he has become the lord of creation. When he is lord also of himself, he will deserve his self-chosen title of *homo sapiens*.
— DEAN WILLIAM R. INGE

A man's conquest of himself dwarfs the ascent of Everest.
— ELI J. SCHIEFER

He that would be superior to external influences must first become superior to his own passions.
— SAMUEL JOHNSON

There is a raging tiger inside every man whom God put on this earth. Every man worthy of the respect of his children spends his life building inside himself a cage to pen that tiger in.
— Murray Kempton

Self-restraint may be alien to the human temperament, but humanity without restraint will dig its own grave.
— Marya Mannes

Self-command is the main elegance.
— Ralph Waldo Emerson

Remember that there is always a limit to self-indulgence, but none to self-restraint.
— Mahatma Gandhi

How shall I be able to rule over others, that have not full power and command of myself?
— Rabelais

Man who man would be,
Must rule the empire of himself.
— Percy Bysshe Shelley

self-reliance

Do not rely completely on any other human being, however
dear. We meet all life's greatest tests alone.
— AGNES MACPHAIL

Our remedies oft in ourselves do lie,
Which we ascribe to heaven.
— WILLIAM SHAKESPEARE

It was on my fifth birthday that Papa put his hand on my
shoulder and said, "Remember, my son, if you ever need
a helping hand, you'll find one at the end of your arm."
— SAM LEVENSON

The future is not in the hands of fate, but in ours.
— JULES JUSSERANO

You've got to do your own growing, no matter how tall your
grandfather was.
— IRISH PROVERB

If you would have a faithful servant, and one that you like,
serve yourself.
— BENJAMIN FRANKLIN

You will not find poetry anywhere unless you bring some of it
with you.
— JOSEPH JOUBERT

There's only one corner of the universe you can be certain of
improving, and that's your own self.
— ALDOUS HUXLEY

If you want a thing done well, do it yourself.
— NAPOLÉON I

I am not afraid of storms, for I am learning how to sail my
ship.
— LOUISA MAY ALCOTT

If there is no wind, row.
— LATIN PROVERB

No bird soars too high, if he soars with his own wings.
— WILLIAM BLAKE

As one goes through life one learns that if you don't paddle
your own canoe, you don't move.
— KATHARINE HEPBURN

Chop your own wood, and it will warm you twice.
— HENRY FORD

No one can really pull you up very high—you lose your grip
on the rope. But on your own two feet you can climb
mountains.
— LOUIS BRANDEIS

Don't wait for your ship to come; swim out to it.
— ANONYMOUS

Parents can only give good advice or put them on the right
paths, but the final forming of a person's character lies in
their own hands.
— ANNE FRANK

They never told me I couldn't.
— TOM DEMPSEY

The only person you can change is yourself.
— MOTTO OF ALCOHOLICS
ANONYMOUS

Temperance

Temperance is the moderating of one's desires in obedience to reason.
— CICERO

We become temperate by abstaining from indulgence, and we are the better able to abstain from indulgence after we have become temperate.
— ARISTOTLE

Choose rather to punish your appetites than to be punished by them.
— TYRIUS MAXIMUS

Temperance is simply a disposition of the mind which sets bounds to the passions.
— THOMAS AQUINAS

Sobriety's a real turn-on for me. You can see what you're doing.
— PETER O'TOOLE

Intemperance is the physician's provider.
— PUBLILIUS SYRUS

Temperance has those advantages over all other means of
health that it may be practised by all ranks and conditions,
at any season, or in any place. It is a kind of regimen into
which every man may put himself, without interruption
to business, expense of money, or loss of time.
— JOSEPH ADDISON

strength

O, do not pray for easy life. Pray to be stronger men. Do not
pray for tasks equal to your powers. Pray for powers
equal to your tasks.
— PHILLIPS BROOKS

A woman is like a tea bag; you don't know her strength until
she is in hot water.
— NANCY REAGAN

Beyond his strength no man can fight, although he be eager.
— HOMER

There are two ways of exerting one's strength: one is pushing
down, the other is pulling up.
— BOOKER T. WASHINGTON

A weak man is just by accident. A strong but nonviolent man
is unjust by accident.
— MAHATMA GANDHI

Neither smiles nor frowns, neither good intentions nor harsh
words, are a substitute for strength.
— JOHN F. KENNEDY

I've never been one who thought the Lord should make life
easy; I've just asked Him to make me strong.
— EVA BOWRING

If you are to be leaders, teachers, and guides among your
people, you must have strength. No people can be fed, no
people can be built up on flowers.
— ALEXANDER CRUMMELL

The first question to be answered by any individual or any
social group, facing a hazardous situation, is whether the
crisis is to be met as a challenge to strength or as an occasion for despair.
— HARRY EMERSON FOSDICK

God is our refuge and strength, a very present help in trouble.
— PSALM 46:1

That man over there says that women need to be helped into carriages, and lifted over ditches, and to have the best place everywhere. Nobody ever helps me into carriages, over mud puddles, or gives me any best place! And ain't I a woman? . . . I have plowed and planted and gathered into barns, and no man could head me—and ain't I a woman? I could work as much and eat as much as a man (when I could get it), and bear the lash as well—and ain't I a woman? I have borne thirteen children and seen them most all sold off into slavery, and when I cried out with a mother's grief, none but Jesus heard—and ain't I a woman?

—Sojourner Truth

Few men during their lifetime come anywhere near exhausting the resources dwelling within them. There are deep wells of strength that are never used.

—Richard E. Byrd

If we are strong, our character will speak for itself. If we are weak, words will be of no help.

—John F. Kennedy

PART XII

WISDOM

This book is subtitled *An Anthology of Wisdom* because that's what it is. And it feels natural to me that its final section should be made up of quotes specifically about wisdom itself.

You will note that this is the only section without subsections—without component virtues. This too is natural. In one sense each and every one of the seventy-eight other virtues in this book is a component of wisdom. And for this reason, in another sense, wisdom belongs in a class of its own: It subsumes all of the other virtues. Wisdom is the number one, the virtue par excellence, the one without equal.

That's a bold statement. "What about love?" you might well ask, and I would agree that it runs a close second. Still, it is second. Love indiscriminately, for instance, and you may well end up causing more harm than good. It is possible to be loving without being wise; it is not possible to be wise without loving.

These quotes about wisdom suffer from the same dilemma as the other virtues: Is wisdom earned or is it a gift? The majority seem to come down in favor of it as earned, or at least as an "earned gift." *Seek* after wisdom, they advise; indeed, seek after it as nothing else, before anything else. Once again, I agree to a certain extent. Deep wisdom must be sought with all our strength. It must be chased down as if our whole life depended upon it. But tell me this: What gives us the wisdom to choose to look for wisdom in the first place? From whence comes the burning desire to make wisdom our primary quest? It is hardly everyone's great goal, and no amount of admonition, such as these quotes, will likely change the fact.

Ultimately, I've come to believe that wisdom (like the other virtues) is more a gift than an earned character trait. I don't mean that it cannot be earned; to the contrary, it must be. I do mean, however, that the origin of the yearning to earn it is obscure and mysterious. Nevertheless, although the "science" of theology will never answer all the questions, I believe it has some big hints to offer.

In the late 1970s, a young woman, Marilyn Von Waldner, then a Catholic nun, composed and sang a collection of twelve Christian songs that were ultimately recorded and published under the title of *What Return Can I Make?* (These songs were so personally powerful that they inspired me to write a book about them.) Two of the twelve songs are specifically about wisdom. The second begins with the resounding proclamation: "Wisdom is a spirit."

Although not spelled out in theological language, what Marilyn meant by being a spirit is that wisdom has its origin in "the Holy Spirit." That term (and its synonym, "the Holy Ghost") will sound like so much gibberish or mumbo jumbo to most nonbelievers. To most educated, devout Christians, however, its meaning is well defined: The Holy Spirit is the part of God that speaks to us directly. Sometimes this spirit—which I sometimes think of as Sophia, after the goddess of wisdom—seems to speak to us through events or coincidences. Most dramatically She can speak to us through certain nighttime dreams (what Carl Jung referred to as "big dreams"). Most commonly She speaks to us through that "still, small voice"—a voice that would seem to come from within our own minds were it not for the fact that, as I've already suggested, its words are far wiser than anything our own brains could cook up.

Space prevents me from recounting (as I have in some of my other, longer books) even a few of my personal encounters with the Holy Spirit, or attempting to explain my total faith in Her and my knowledge that Her gentle urging is the origin of wisdom. Let me simply state that the more I have wondered at the Holy Spirit the more I have been pushed to confront glory. Marilyn is also quite clear in her song that we need to actively seek the Holy Spirit, that we are not mere passive partners in the dance. Later in her song, however, she exalts in the fact that if you yearn and seek after the Holy Spirit in your life, then "the Lord will give you His mind." I know of no sentence in all of literature that so directly speaks to the human potential for glory. Actively seek wisdom from its font, the Holy Spirit, and it will upon occasion actually be possible for you to think with the mind of God!

This still begs the question of why or how it is that most do not attempt to thoroughly ally themselves with the mind of God, of why they have either never heard the voice of the Holy Spirit or recognized it as such. Several sections back I suggested this might be because they deliberately "left the phone off the hook." Yet why, again? There I quoted St. Paul as saying, "It is a terrifying thing to fall into the hands of the living God," alluding to the loss (or sense of loss) of control involved. In the Introduction to Part XI, I began to approach the same issue from a slightly different angle. Within the confines of the subject of strength I suggested that it is within our power or human strength to decide the kind of God we are going to believe in.

It was a radical thing to suggest . . . almost deviant. Our traditional notion is that God is all-powerful; that, whether we like it or not, we are His to mold; that God is what He is, and that although we may reject Him, it is certainly not in our puny, mortal human power to fashion Him. But I am not so sure about this. We may not be able to change the nature of God to suit our fancy, but I can tell you for sure that a change in our understanding of the nature of God will change us, change those around us, and hence change the world, no matter how minusculely.

I have said that God speaks to us through His or Her Holy Spirit in order to offer us wisdom. If we believe this, we are much less likely to leave the phone off the hook. But if we believe God does not speak to us, there's no point in even having that kind of phone or thinking that whatever wisdom we might possess is anything other than our own.

What kind of God do we want? One who speaks to us? One who is forever aloof? Or one who doesn't exist at all? Certain things, among them good or bad childhood experiences, may influence this choice, but never totally determine it. Whether we care for the responsibility or not, the choice is still ours.

Many questions remain, and I have only little hints. If there is a God . . . and if She does communicate with us . . . why should She be so interested in helping us toward wisdom?

In the long run I have nothing new to say. I never have had. Just a few new ways of saying it. I thought it would be nice to end this final introduction with something about wisdom that was profoundly new and profoundly my own. But that was not the way the Holy Spirit chose to work. Instead, my inspiration has been corny and provincial.

There is a current, relatively recent weekly TV program entitled *Touched by an Angel*. Each episode centers around one or more people who are deeply troubled and a whole slew of angels God has sent to give them wisdom—a wisdom they generally don't want. Toward the end of each episode one of the angels (who looks as human as the rest of us) counters the character's resistance to the wisdom they offer by flatly stating: "I am an angel, sent to you by God because God wants you to know that He loves you." Through this they teach the character how important he or she is.

I could go on and on and on about wisdom. The subject excites me as no other. But in the end the most significant thing I have to point you in the path toward wisdom is to tell you that "God wants you to know that He loves you."

wisdom

Knowledge is proud that he has learned so much;
Wisdom is humble that he knows no more.
— WILLIAM COWPER

I don't think much of a man who is not wiser today than he
was yesterday.
— ABRAHAM LINCOLN

Every man is a damn fool for at least five minutes every day.
Wisdom consists in not exceeding the limit.
— ELBERT HUBBARD

I do not believe that sheer suffering teaches. If suffering alone
taught, all the world would be wise, since everyone suffers. To suffering must be added mourning, understanding, patience, love, openness, and the willingness to
remain vulnerable.
— ANNE MORROW LINDBERGH

Men who love wisdom should acquaint themselves with a
great many particulars.
— HERACLITUS

Wisdom consists not so much in knowing what to do in the ultimate as in knowing what to do next.
— HERBERT HOOVER

Many persons are both wise and handsome—but they would probably be still wiser were they less handsome.
— TALMUD

It is easier to be wise on behalf of others than to be so for ourselves.
— LA ROCHEFOUCAULD

Wisdom never lies.
— HOMER

Youth is the time to study wisdom; old age is the time to practice it.
— JEAN-JACQUES ROUSSEAU

There are two sentences inscribed upon the Delphic oracle ... : "Know thyself" and "Nothing too much" and upon these all other precepts depend.
— PLUTARCH

Through wisdom a house is built and through understanding
it is established.
— PROVERBS 24:3

Who is wise? He that learns from everyone.
— BENJAMIN FRANKLIN

The fool doth think he is wise, but the wise man knows himself to be a fool.
— WILLIAM SHAKESPEARE

Wisdom is ofttimes nearer when we stoop
Than when we soar.
— WILLIAM WORDSWORTH

Wisdom denotes the pursuing of the best ends by the best
means.
— FRANCES HUTCHESON

The wise man forgets insults as the ungrateful forget benefits.
— CHINESE PROVERB

The clouds may drop down titles and estates;
Wealth may seek us; but wisdom must be sought.
— EDWARD YOUNG

He who has imagination without learning has wings but no
feet.
— FRENCH PROVERB

Our wisest reflections (if the word wise may be given to
humanity) are tainted by our hopes and fears.
— MARY WORTLEY MONTAGU

It requires wisdom to understand wisdom; the music is nothing if the audience is deaf.
— WALTER LIPPMANN

A wise man, to accomplish his end, may even carry his foe on
his shoulder.
— PANCHATANTRA

Wisdom is divided into two parts: (a) having a great deal to
say, and (b) not saying it.
— ANONYMOUS

Those who wish to appear wise among fools, among the wise
seem foolish.
— QUINTILLIAN

Common sense in an uncommon degree is what the world
calls wisdom.
— ANONYMOUS

To know one's self is wisdom, but to know one's neighbor is
genius.
— ANNA ANDRIM

A man's wisdom is most conspicuous where he is able to distinguish among dangers and make choice of the least.
— MACHIAVELLI

Wisdom is not to be obtained from textbooks, but must be
coined out of human experience in the flame of life.
— MORRIS RAPHAEL COHEN

Knowledge can be communicated, but not wisdom. One can
find it, live it, be fortified by it, do wonders through it,
but one cannot communicate and teach it.
— HERMANN HESSE

Wisdom is an affair of values, and of value judgments. It is intelligent conduct of human affairs.
—SYDNEY HOOK

Old places and old persons in their turn, when spirit dwells in them, have an intrinsic vitality of which youth is incapable; precisely the balance and wisdom that comes from long perspectives and broad foundations.
—GEORGE SANTAYANA

Knowledge alone is not enough. It must be leavened with magnanimity before it becomes wisdom.
—ADLAI E. STEVENSON

The art of being wise is the art of knowing what to overlook.
—WILLIAM JAMES

Common sense is not so common.
—VOLTAIRE

The eyes are of little use if the mind be blind.
—ARAB PROVERB

All wisdom comes from the Lord,
And remains with him forever.
The sand of the seas, and the drops of rain,
And the days of eternity—who can count them?
The height of the heavens, and the breadth of the earth,
And the deep, and wisdom—who can track them out?
Wisdom was created before them all,
And sound intelligence from eternity.
— BEN SIRA

Wonder is the beginning of wisdom.
— GREEK PROVERB

There is no purifier in this world equal to wisdom.
— BHAGAVAD GITA

Not to know is bad, but not to wish to know is worse.
— WEST AFRICAN PROVERB

To know how to grow old is the master-work of wisdom, and
one of the most difficult chapters in the great art of living.
— HENRI FRÉDÉRIC AMIEL

A questioning man is halfway to being wise.
— IRISH PROVERB

The function of wisdom is to discriminate between good and
    evil.
                — CICERO

The doorstep to the temple of wisdom is a knowledge of our
    own ignorance.
                — C. H. SPURGEON

If one is too lazy to think, too vain to do a thing badly, too
    cowardly to admit it, one will never attain wisdom.
                — CYRIL CONNOLLY

So teach us to number our days, that we may apply our hearts
    unto wisdom.
                — PSALM 90:12

If there were wisdom in beards, all goats would be prophets.
                — ARMENIAN PROVERB

When you have got an elephant by the hind legs and he is try-
    ing to run away, it's best to let him run.
                — ABRAHAM LINCOLN

Pain makes man think. Thought makes man wise. Wisdom
makes life endurable.
— JOHN PATRICK

Great wisdom consists in not demanding too much of human
nature, and yet not altogether spoiling it by indulgence.
— LIN YUTANG

He is a wise man who does not grieve for the things which he
has not, but rejoices for those which he has.
— EPICTETUS

In seeking wisdom, thou art wise; in imagining that thou hast
attained it, thou art a fool.
— BEN SIRA

It is unwise to be too sure of one's own wisdom. It is healthy
to be reminded that the strongest might weaken and the
wisest might err.
— MAHATMA GANDHI

Wisdom is knowing what to do next;
Skill is knowing how to do it, and Virtue is doing it.
— DAVID STARR JORDAN

A man cannot leave his wisdom or his experience to his heirs.
— ITALIAN PROVERB

Many persons might have attained to wisdom had they not
assumed that they already possessed it.
— SENECA

Money does not prevent you from becoming lame.
You may be ill in any part of your body,
So it is better for you to go and think again
And to select wisdom.
— IFA YORUBAN

Seven characteristics distinguish the wise: he does not speak
in the presence of one wiser than himself, does not interrupt, is not hasty to answer, asks and answers the point,
talks about first things first and about last things last,
admits when he does not know, and acknowledges the
truth.
— TALMUD

The man who views the world at fifty the same as he did at
twenty has wasted thirty years of his life.
— MUHAMMAD ALI

The first dawn of smartness is to stop trying things you don't
know anything about—especially if they run to anything
over a dollar.
— WILSON MIZNER

At twenty-two, I thought I knew everything. Now, at sixty-
seven, I find I haven't tasted a drop from the sea of
knowledge. The more I learn, the more I find out how
little I know.
— JOHN COPAGE

A man doesn't begin to attain wisdom until he recognizes that
he is no longer indispensable.
— ADMIRAL BYRD

To wisdom belongs the intellectual apprehension of eternal things;
to knowledge, the rational knowledge of temporal things.
— SAINT AUGUSTINE

It may be a mistake to mix different wines, but old and new
wisdom mix admirably.
— BERTOLT BRECHT

Not to know certain things is a great part of wisdom.
— HUGO GROTIUS

Wisdom is ever a blessing; education is sometimes a curse.
— JOHN A. SHEDD

The road to wisdom? Well, it's plain
And simple to express;
Err
And err
And err again
But less
And less
And less.

— PIET HEIN

A wise man hears one word and understands two.
— JEWISH PROVERB

Almost every wise saying has an opposite one, no less wise, to
balance it.
— GEORGE SANTAYANA

It's taken me all my life to understand that it is not necessary
to understand everything.
— RENÉ COTY

He is no wise man that cannot play the fool upon occasion.
— THOMAS FULLER, M.D.

What a man knows at fifty that he did not know at twenty is
for the most part incommunicable.
— ADLAI E. STEVENSON

Nine-tenths of wisdom consists in being wise in time.
— THEODORE ROOSEVELT

To have lived long does not necessarily imply the gathering of
much wisdom and experience. A man who has pedaled
twenty-five thousand miles on a stationary bicycle has
not circled the globe. He has only garnered weariness.
— PAUL ELDRIDGE

To know when to be generous and when firm—this is wisdom.
— ELBERT HUBBARD

The seat of knowledge is in the head; of wisdom, in the heart.
We are sure to judge wrong if we do not feel right.
— WILLIAM HAZLITT